SECRETS OF CAMP WHATEVER

By CHRIS GRINE

Designed by KATE Z. STONE
Edited by SHAWNA GORE
Consulting Reader ALEXANDREA GILL

AN ONI PRESS PUBLICATION

PUBLISHED BY ONI-LION FORGE PUBLISHING GROUP, LLC

onipress.com
facebook.com/onipress
twitter.com/onipress
instagram.com/onipress

lionforge.com
facebook.com/lionforge
twitter.com/lionforge
instagram.com/lionforge

Chrisgrine.com
instagram.com/grinetastic
twitter.com/chrisgrine

First edition: March 2021

ISBN 978-1-62010-862-8
eISBN 978-1-62010-863-5

PRINTED IN CHINA

Library of Congress Control Number:2020940922

1 3 5 7 9 10 8 6 4 2

SECRETS OF CAMP WHATEVER

WHY CAN'T I GO TO SUMMER CAMP, TOO? IT'S NOT FAIR WILLOW GETS TO GO HAVE FUN AND I DON'T.
SORRY, *MIJO*. IT DOESN'T WORK THAT WAY. BESIDES, YOU HAVE A WHOLE NEW HOUSE TO EXPLORE.
HEY, WIL, DID YOU REMEMBER EVERYTHING?
WE WERE RUNNING LATE THIS MORNING SINCE THE ALARM CLOCKS ALL VERY **MYSTERIOUSLY** WENT MISSING.
Welcome to
NOWHERE
est. 1882?
I **WONDER** HOW THEY ENDED UP BEHIND THE COUCH LIKE THAT?
IT'S **ALMOST** LIKE SOMEONE WAS **TRYING** TO STOP US FROM GOING SOMEWHERE.
WIL? WILLOW?
GRYPHIN, GET YOUR SISTER'S ATTENTION. SHE MUST HAVE HER HEARING AIDS TURNED OFF.

WAKEY, WAKEY!
TURN ON YOUR EARS!
HEY!

MOM TOLD ME TO DO IT! IT WAS HER IDEA!

TURN ON YOUR HEARING AIDS.

CLICK
YOUR DAD WANTS TO KNOW IF YOU PACKED THE BUG SPRAY AND A FLASHLIGHT.
YES.
AND EXTRA BATTERIES FOR YOUR HEARING AIDS?
THEY'RE IN WITH MY SNACKS.
OH, I FORGOT TO TELL YOU, WHEN I WAS ENROLLING YOU IN YOUR NEW MIDDLE SCHOOL, THE LADY IN THE OFFICE TOLD ME THE CAMP'S NURSE KNOWS SOME SIGN LANGUAGE. THAT'S KINDA COOL, RIGHT?
HOW DOES **SHE** KNOW?
SMALL TOWN, I GUESS.
DID SHE SAY WHY IT'S CALLED CAMP...WHATEVER?
WAIT...DOES THIS PLACE EVEN **HAVE** A NAME?

THAT'S A STORY YOU'LL LEARN AROUND THE CAMPFIRE TONIGHT!

AT LEAST, THAT'S HOW THEY DID IT WHEN I WENT THERE.

THAT WAS A **MILLION** YEARS AGO, DAD.

I **KNOW** YOU'RE NOT SUPER EXCITED, WIL, BUT IT'LL BE **AMAZING**. I PROMISE.

THAT'S WHAT YOU SAID WHEN GRYPHIN WAS BORN.

WELL, REGARDLESS, WE'RE GOING TO HAVE A **PARADE** OF CONTRACTORS AND WORKERS IN AND OUT ALL WEEK.
IT'LL JUST BE EASIER FOR ME AND YOUR DAD IF WE ONLY HAVE **ONE** ROTTEN CHILD TO DEAL WITH.
THERE'S A LITTLE DINER UP AHEAD. WHO'S HUNGRY?
WHAT IF I **PROMISED** TO STAY IN MY ROOM ALL WEEK?
NICE TRY, GIRLFRIEND, BUT NO DICE.
PANCAKES!
THIS PLACE BETTER HAVE COFFEE.
CHICKEN & HARE Diner
CHICKEN & HARE Diner

CHICKEN & HARE Diner

MORNIN', FOLKS, WHAT CAN I GET STARTED FOR YA?

CHICKEN & HARE Diner

COFFEE FOR US, THANKS.

WIL?

GRYPHIN'S BEING SO **GROSS**.

SHE'LL HAVE COFFEE, ALSO. AND CHOCOLATE MILK FOR HIM.

OH, AND HE'LL NEED A STRAW.

IS THAT RIGHT? I BET YOU'RE EXCITED.
THRILLED.

YOU FOLKS NOT FROM AROUND HERE, THEN?
WE'RE MOVING INTO MY HUSBAND'S LATE GRANDMOTHER'S PLACE OUT ON THE EDGE OF TOWN.
IT'S THE OLD VICTORIAN JUST PAST TROLL'S BRIDGE.

OH DEAR... YOU FOLKS LOOK LIKE A NICE FAMILY, SO, LET ME GIVE YOU SOME FREE ADVICE.
Y'ALL GET IN YOUR CAR, TURN AROUND, AND GO **BACK** TO WHEREVER YOU CAME FROM.
THEY SAY THAT HOUSE AND THEM HILLS ARE **HAUNTED**, AND I BELIEVE 'EM.

EXCUSE ME?

NOW, MILLY, DON'T GO **SCARIN'** THESE NICE PEOPLE.

SORRY, FISH. I'LL BE RIGHT BACK WITH YOUR DRINKS, FOLKS.

OVERHEARD YA SAY YOU MOVED INTO THE MILVAR PLACE.

I'M SHERIFF FISHER, BUT THE LOCALS JUST CALL ME FISH.

GOOD TO MEET YOU, SHERIFF.

I'M JUSTIN AND THIS IS MY WIFE, ELENA, AND OUR KIDS, WILLOW AND GRYPHIN.

NOW, FISH, DON'T YOU GO SCARIN' THESE NICE FOLKS, **TOO.** SHEESH.

HI, I'M HENRY PERSON. I RUN THE NOWHERE MUSEUM AND GIFT SHOP.

OH, IS NOWHERE KNOWN FOR ANYTHING?

INDEED IT **IS**! OUR LITTLE TOWN IS HOME TO **MANY** A STRANGE TALE, MA'AM.

THIS PLACE IS ABOUT AS MYSTERIOUS AS THEY COME. SOME PEOPLE **CLAIM** TO HAVE SEEN **GIANT** SERPENTS IN THE LAKE AND ELVES IN THE FOREST. OTHERS CLAIM TO HAVE SPOTTED THE LEGENDARY **BIGFOOT** NEAR THE SHORE OR HEARD MERMAIDS LAUGHING.

NONE OF IT CAN BE CONFIRMED, OF COURSE, BECAUSE THAT **DARN** FOG IS JUST TOO THICK TO SEE INTO, AS I'M SURE YOU'VE NOTICED...

A LOCAL FELLA NAMED JIMMY DUNN WENT A-SNEAKIN' 'ROUND THAT ISLAND WHERE THE SUMMER CAMP'S LOCATED LOOKIN' FOR THE SASQUATCH YEARS AGO.
THEY SAY HE EVEN FOUND IT. ALL WE KNOW FOR SURE IS SOMETHING OVER THERE SCARED JIMMY SO BAD THAT NIGHT HE AIN'T BEEN RIGHT IN THE HEAD SINCE.

AND...THERE'S A SUMMER CAMP THERE FOR...**CHILDREN**? HOW IS THAT **SAFE**?
SEE! WE SHOULD GO HOME.
HEH...THE SUMMER I ATTENDED WE ACTUALLY HAD A CAMPER GO MISSING, AND AS FAR AS I KNOW, THEY **NEVER** FOUND HIM.
AND YOU'RE JUST TELLING ME THIS **NOW**, JUSTIN?
WE'RE SENDING OUR DAUGHTER TO A SUMMER CAMP WHERE CHILDREN HAVE GONE **MISSING**, AND THERE COULD BE **DANGEROUS** ANIMALS RUNNING WILD?
OH MY, YOU WERE HERE IN THAT YEAR, EH?
I WOULD LIKE TO INTERVIEW YOU ABOUT THAT SUMMER, IF YOU GET A SPARE MOMENT SOMETIME.
SURE, I GUESS. I DON'T REALLY REMEMBER MUCH TO BE HONEST.
IN LIGHT OF **CERTAIN** INFO YOU'VE WAITED UNTIL **JUST NOW** TO SHARE, MAYBE WE **SHOULD** RECONSIDER THIS CAMP.
WE **TOTALLY** SHOULD.

THAT ISLAND'S PRETTY BIG, BUT FROM WHAT I KNOW, THEY KEEP THE KIDS TOGETHER IN CAMP, AND THEY'RE MONITORED AT ALL TIMES.
IT'S SAFE ENOUGH. BESIDES, THEY GOT THEMSELVES A NEW CAMP DIRECTOR THIS YEAR, CLARENCE TOOTER.
HE'S A WORLD-CLASS, BIG GAME HUNTER. IF ANYONE CAN KEEP THE CAMPERS SAFE, IT'LL BE HIM.
OH, DID MRS. CALDEN FINALLY RETIRE?
NOPE. SHE'S DEAD.
OH...
SOME SAY SHE WAS MESSING WITH THINGS SHE OUGHT NOT HAVE BEEN MESSIN' WITH.
THAT WOMAN WAS A WITCH IF EVER I'VE SEEN ONE.

BET SHE PUT A SPELL ON...
NOW, HENRY, DON'T YOU GO **SCARIN'** THESE FOLKS WITH YOUR WITCHY TALES OF BIGFEETS AND VAMPIRES. FOR HEAVEN'S SAKE, THEY'VE **ALREADY** GOT A **MAJOR** GHOST PROBLEM.

VAMPIRES AND WITCHES? GIVE ME A BREAK.

WHY DON'T YOU STOP BY THE MUSEUM SOMETIME? I'LL SHOW YOU SOME ARTIFACTS THAT MIGHT CHANGE YOUR MIND, YOUNG LADY.

I HAVE A PLASTER CAST OF A SASQUATCH FOOTPRINT, A CONCRETE GNOME COVERED IN STRANGE RUNES, AND A GHOST TRAPPED IN A JAR-- JUST TO NAME A FEW!

SHOO, HENRY. THESE FOLKS ARE HUNGRY AND WOULD LIKE TO EAT.
ANOTHER TIME, PERHAPS. ENJOY YOUR BREAKFAST.

THIRTY MINUTES LATER
CHICKEN & HARE Diner
WELL, I'M STUFFED.
WE'D BETTER GET GOING. YOUR BOAT LEAVES IN ABOUT TWENTY-FIVE MINUTES, WIL.
BUT, I'M SO SCARED NOW. WHAT IF BIGFOOT EATS ME, OR WHAT IF A WITCH PUTS A SPELL ON ME?
MAYBE I SHOULD JUST GO WITH YOU GUYS AND HELP UNPACK?
IT'LL BE GOOD FOR YOU, WIL.
MAYBE YOU'LL MAKE SOME FRIENDS BEFORE SCHOOL STARTS UP THIS FALL.
OR MAYBE I'LL BE TURNED INTO A VAMPIRE, AND I WON'T NEED TO GO TO SCHOOL. I GUESS THAT MIGHT BE NICE.
YOU ALWAYS FIND THE SILVER LINING.

GAH!
ARE YOU MARKED WITH A STAR, CHILD?

EXCUSE ME?

YOUR DAUGHTER, DOES SHE HAVE ANY TYPE OF MARKING THAT RESEMBLES A STAR?
A BIRTHMARK, PERHAPS?

OKAY, HENRY, IT'S TIME YOU LEFT THESE NICE FOLKS ALONE, SO THEY CAN BE ON THEIR WAY NOW.

YOU FOLKS HAVE A NICE DAY.

SUPER COOL TOWN YOU MOVED US TO, DAD.

I'LL ADMIT BREAKFAST WENT A LITTLE SIDEWAYS ON US, BUT COME ON, WIL, YOU'LL LOVE NOWHERE ONCE YOU GET TO KNOW IT BETTER.

YOU'RE GONNA HAVE SO MUCH FUN THIS WEEK.
I'LL GLADLY TRADE PLACES WITH ANYONE WHO WANTS TO TO TAKE MY SPOT AT CAMP CREEPY...OR WHATEVER.

THIS PLACE IS SO WEIRD, DAD.
YOU HAVE NO IDEA.

EXCUSE ME, SIR. THIS IS OUR FIRST TIME AT SUMMER CAMP. ARE WE IN THE RIGHT SPOT?

WELCOME TO CAMP...WHATEVER! SHE'S GONNA **LOVE** IT!

THAT'S WHAT I WAS **JUST** TELLING HER.

HE'S GONNA **LOVE** IT!

UH...WELL, IT'S ONLY OUR DAUGHTER GOING, BUT I'M SURE SHE WILL.

CAN I HAVE A BALLOON?
YOU'RE GONNA **LOVE** IT!
SO, IS UH...IS THAT WHERE WE SIGN HER IN?
YOU'RE GONNA **LOVE** IT!
THANKS... FOR YOUR HELP?

IS THAT GUY EVEN PART OF THE CAMP STAFF?
YIKES! STRIKE TWO FOR CREEPY-TOWN, DAD.

AMOR, WHY DON'T YOU TAKE THE KIDS OVER TO LOOK AT THE BOAT. I'LL CHECK HER IN.

IT'LL SAVE SOME TIME.
GOOD THINKING.

AMAZING! I THINK THIS IS THE SAME BOAT THEY USED WHEN I CAME HERE.
WHATCHA' THINKIN', KID?

I'M THINKING IT'S A GOOD THING THIS FOG IS SO THICK.
IT HIDES THE HOLES.

SHE'S MUCH FASTER THAN SHE LOOKS, I ASSURE YOU. BROUGHT HER OVER MYSELF THIS MORNING.
AND CONSIDERING SHE'S OLDER THAN ANYONE CAN REMEMBER, THAT IS QUITE AN ACHIEVEMENT.
I GUESS THEY JUST DON'T MAKE 'EM LIKE THIS ANYMORE.
IS THIS YOUR FIRST YEAR AT CAMP...WHATEVER?
UH... YEAH.
IT'S MINE, AS WELL. I'M MR. TOOTER, THE NEW CAMP DIRECTOR.
AND YOU ARE...?

THIS IS MY DAUGHTER, WILLOW.

SO, THIS IS WILLOW? OUR FIRST **DEAF** CAMPER.
ACTUALLY, SHE CAN...

WELCOME TO CAMP, WILLOW.
YOUR HAIR IS PURPLE.

THERE'S NO NEED TO SHOUT, MR. TOOTER.
WILLOW'S HEARING AIDS ALLOW HER TO--

OKAY.

OKAY, WIL. YOU'RE ALL SET, KIDDO.
HEY, WAS THAT THE NEW CAMP LEADER TALKING TO YOU?
DID HE SEEM NICE?
GUYS?
DID I **MISS** SOMETHING?
I FEEL LIKE I **MISSED** SOMETHING.
TRY NOT TO LOOK SO **EXCITED**, WIL.
YEAH, MAYBE DIAL IT BACK A LITTLE.
THERE'S THAT **BEAUTIFUL** SMILE.
I'M HAVING RESERVATIONS ABOUT THIS PLACE.
JUST KEEP SMILING. SHE'LL BE FINE.

I JUST KEEP THINKING ABOUT THAT MISSING CAMPER. AREN'T YOU WORRIED ABOUT THAT?
HAVE YOU **MET** OUR DAUGHTER? I'M MORE WORRIED ABOUT WHAT **SHE'S** GOING TO DO TO THAT CAMP.

SHE'S GONNA HAVE AN **AMAZING** WEEK, TRUST ME.

AND LOOK, BY THE TIME CAMP IS OVER WE'LL HAVE UNPACKED MOST OF THE NEW HOUSE.

AND WITH SOME LUCK, GOTTEN RID OF ALL THE **GHOSTS** IN THE CELLAR.

GULP.

WELCOME, CAMPERS. PLEASE FIND SEATS QUICKLY AS WE'LL BE PICKING UP SPEED SHORTLY, AND IT TENDS TO BE A LITTLE BUMPY.

PLEASE MAKE ROOM FOR OTHERS.
NO SAVING SEATS.

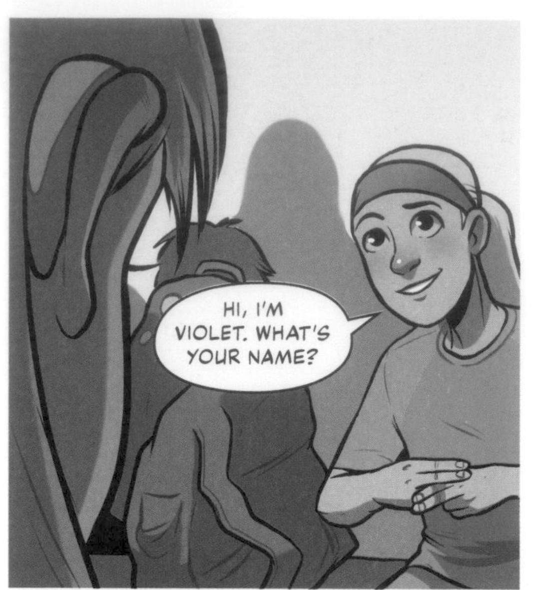
HI, I'M VIOLET. WHAT'S YOUR NAME?

I'M WILLOW... YOU KNOW SIGN LANGUAGE?

KINDA. MY COUSIN JENNY TAUGHT ME A LITTLE.
I SAW YOUR HEARING AIDS. I HOPE I'M NOT BEING RUDE. I JUST THOUGHT...
NO. IT'S COOL.

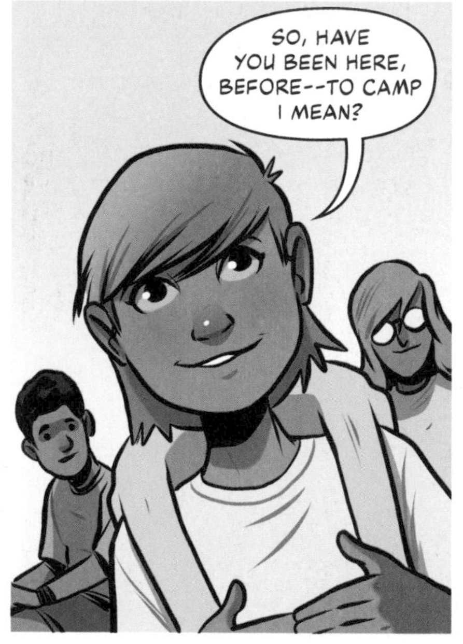
SO, HAVE YOU BEEN HERE, BEFORE--TO CAMP I MEAN?

NOPE. FIRST TIME. I'VE HEARD IT'S EVEN STRANGER THAN THE TOWN.

DID YOU SEE THE DUDE WITH THE BALLOONS?

UH, **YES!** MY MOM TRIED TO ASK HIM DIRECTIONS.
SO DID MY DAD.

WELL, I GUESS WE'RE GONNA LOVE IT!

HA HA HA HA HA
ARE YOU GUYS TALKING ABOUT THE CLOWN GUY?
HE WAS **SO** FREAKY.

HEY, NICE FLOWER. DIDN'T THEY HAVE ANYTHING BIGGER?

SWIPE

CRUNCH

YOU'RE IN OUR SEATS.

C'MON, KURT, THERE'S PLENTY OF OTHER SEATS. NO NEED TO BE RUDE.
YOU GONNA **MAKE** ME, RAND?

IT'S OKAY, WE'LL MOVE. BUT FIRST, YOU HAVE TO TELL ME HOW MUCH YOU PAID YOUR BARBER TO MAKE YOU LOOK LIKE A **SKUNK.**

YOU THINK THAT'S **FUNNY**?
IT WAS OKAY. NOT MY BEST WORK.

C'MON, SHE DIDN'T MEAN IT.
YOU GONNA SPRAY ME, STINKY?
I HATE SKUNKS!

STAY OUTTA THIS, RAND.
SLAP
CALL ME **STINKY** AGAIN.
C'MON, GUYS. THERE'S BETTER SEATS IN THE BACK, ANYWAY.

WHAT'S THE MATTER, YOU **SCARED** TO HIT A **GIRL**?

OR ARE YOU SCARED SHE MIGHT **HIT** YOU **BACK**?

I DON'T HIT DISABLED KIDS.

IT'S BAD LUCK OR SOMETHING.

I'LL DISABLE YOUR FACE.

LET'S ALL TAKE OUR SEATS. WE'RE MAKING OUR WAY TO CAMP PRESENTLY.

THAT'S JUST KURT. HE'S MY OLDER BROTHER.
HE'S NOT SO BAD...MOST OF THE TIME.

I BET WE CAN FIND YOU A NEW FLOWER FOR YOUR HAIR WHEN WE GET TO CAMP.
IT'S OKAY, IT WOULDN'T HAVE LASTED MUCH LONGER, ANYWAY.

UH...THERE'S NO SAIL, OR ANY OARS FOR ROWING, RIGHT?
HOW IS THIS BOAT MOVING?

MY SISTER TOLD ME IT'S ON A TRACK LIKE AT AN AMUSEMENT PARK, BUT YOU CAN'T SEE IT BECAUSE THAT PART'S UNDERWATER.

I GUESS THAT MAKES SENSE.

BOOM

DID WE **HIT** SOMETHING.
PROBABLY JUST THE ENGINE TURNING ON.

THE BREEZE IS NICE.

THIS THING CAN REALLY MOVE.

SOON
ATTENTION, CAMPERS.
PLEASE DISEMBARK SINGLE FILE AND FOLLOW THE COUNSELORS ONTO THE ISLAND AND UP THE PATH.
FOR YOUR OWN SAFETY, PLEASE STAY ON ON THE PATH.

SOMEONE SPENT A **LOT** OF MONEY ON GARDEN GNOMES.
THEY LOOK **REALLY** CREEPY IN THE FOG LIKE THAT.

UH...THEY'RE NOT WAITING FOR US.
WE'LL CATCH UP IN A MINUTE, VIOLET. COME ON.

I THINK THIS IS WRITING, OR SOMETHING.
WHAT DO YOU THINK IT SAYS?
SOMETHING ABOUT NEEDING MORE BUG SPRAY, PROBABLY.

SO ODD.

FEELS LIKE THE FOG IS WATCHING US. WE SHOULD GO.
RELAX, VIOLET.

WE NEED TO CATCH UP WITH THE GROUP, WIL. WE'RE NOT EVEN SUPPOSED TO BE DOWN HERE.
WHAT IF SOMETHING HAPPENS?
IT'S SUMMER CAMP, VIOLET, FOR KIDS. WHAT'S THE **WORST** THAT CAN HAPPEN?
YOU WOULD BE SURPRISED, CHILD, THE DANGERS THAT SURROUND YOU ON THIS ISLAND.
THESE WOODS ARE FULL OF EYES. MOST ARE BENIGN, BUT **NOT** ALL.
GO NOW. RETURN TO YOUR GROUP, AND SEE THAT YOU **DON'T** STRAY OFF THE PATH AGAIN--FOR YOUR OWN SAFETY.
YOU'VE BEEN MORE FORTUNATE THAN YOU REALIZE SO CLOSE TO THE WATER'S EDGE.
WHAT...? WHAT'S IN THE...WATER?
GO!

WHAT DO YOU THINK'S IN THE WATER?
I **DON'T** CARE.

CAMP
EST. 1902
...AND THOSE ARE THE RULES.
GREAT, WE **MISSED** THE RULES.

NOW, **EACH** OF YOU HAVE BEEN ASSIGNED TO ONE OF **SIX** CABINS UP AHEAD.
THESE INCLUDE MERMAID, UNICORN, FROG, SASQUATCH, GNOME, AND SKUNK. FOUR CAMPERS AND ONE COUNSELOR PER CABIN.
CABIN ASSIGNMENTS ARE POSTED ON THE DOORS, SO GO FIND YOUR NAME, DROP OFF YOUR BAGS, CHANGE INTO YOUR **YELLOW** CAMP SHIRTS, AND TAKE A FEW MINUTES TO GET TO KNOW YOUR BUNKMATES. BE BACK OUT HERE IN **FIFTEEN** MINUTES.

HEY, EMMA. WHAT DID WE MISS?
UH...PRETTY MUCH THE **SCARIEST** LIST OF RULES I'VE **EVER** HEARD.

REALLY? LIKE WHAT, DON'T EAT THE COOKING?

LIKE, WE **GET** TO GO SWIMMING BUT NO DEEPER THAN OUR **KNEES,** OR SOMETHING COULD **GET** US.
OR MY **FAVORITE**--TRY TO AVOID THE DENSER PATCHES OF FOG **ESPECIALLY** AFTER DARK BECAUSE SOMETHING MIGHT **GET** US.

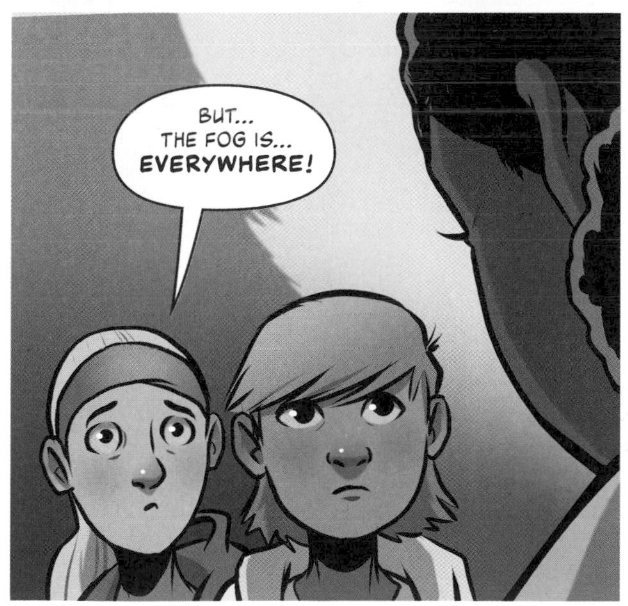
BUT... THE FOG IS... **EVERYWHERE!**

I KNOW!
I'M KINDA TERRIFIED.

I'M BEGINNING TO THINK MY MOM WAS RIGHT ABOUT THIS PLACE NOT BEING APPROPRIATE FOR KIDS.
DON'T FORGET ABOUT THE **LEECHES**.

LEECHES?
FOG LEECHES.

THERE'S...
LEECHES...
...IN FOG?
FOG LEECHES?
NO, VIOLET. SHE'S MESSING WITH YOU.
AM I?

WELL?
ARE WE CABINMATES?
YEP!
ALSO EMMA.
AND SOMEONE NAMED MOLLY.
WHO'S MOLLY?
I'M MOLLY.
DID I HEAR MY NAME?

ANYONE CARE IF I GRAB A TOP BUNK?
DO IT.
DO YOU GUYS THINK WE'LL GET TO SWIM TODAY?
THAT'S WHAT I'M THE **MOST** EXCITED ABOUT DOING.
HOPEFULLY NOTHING **GETS** YOU.
PERSONALLY, I CAN'T WAIT FOR **CRAFT TIME!**
MAYBE WE'LL GET TO MAKE SUN-CATCHERS!
YES!
COOL! WELL, DON'T WAIT FOR ME. I HAVE TO DO A FEW THINGS, AND THEN I'LL BE RIGHT BEHIND YOU.

WELCOME CAMPER
WELCOME TO CAMP...WHATEVER! MY NAME IS MR. CLARENCE TOOTER, AND I'M IN CHARGE.
THE PEOPLE STANDING UP HERE WITH ME ARE YOUR COUNSELORS AND THEY'LL BE DOING...WHATEVER IT IS THEY DO.
BE ADVISED THAT I DON'T LIKE CHILDREN, AND I'LL BE DOING MY VERY BEST TO AVOID ALL OF YOU.
NOW, SUMMER CAMP OR NOT, THERE IS TO BE NO UNAUTHORIZED HIKING OR EXPLORING IN THE FOREST.
IT IS NO DOUBT FILLED WITH ANGRY, WILD ANIMALS THAT MIGHT WANT TO EAT YOU, AND I CAN'T STAND CRYING KIDS.
HEY, WHERE'S WILLOW?
RESTROOM?
HMM.
MAYBE...

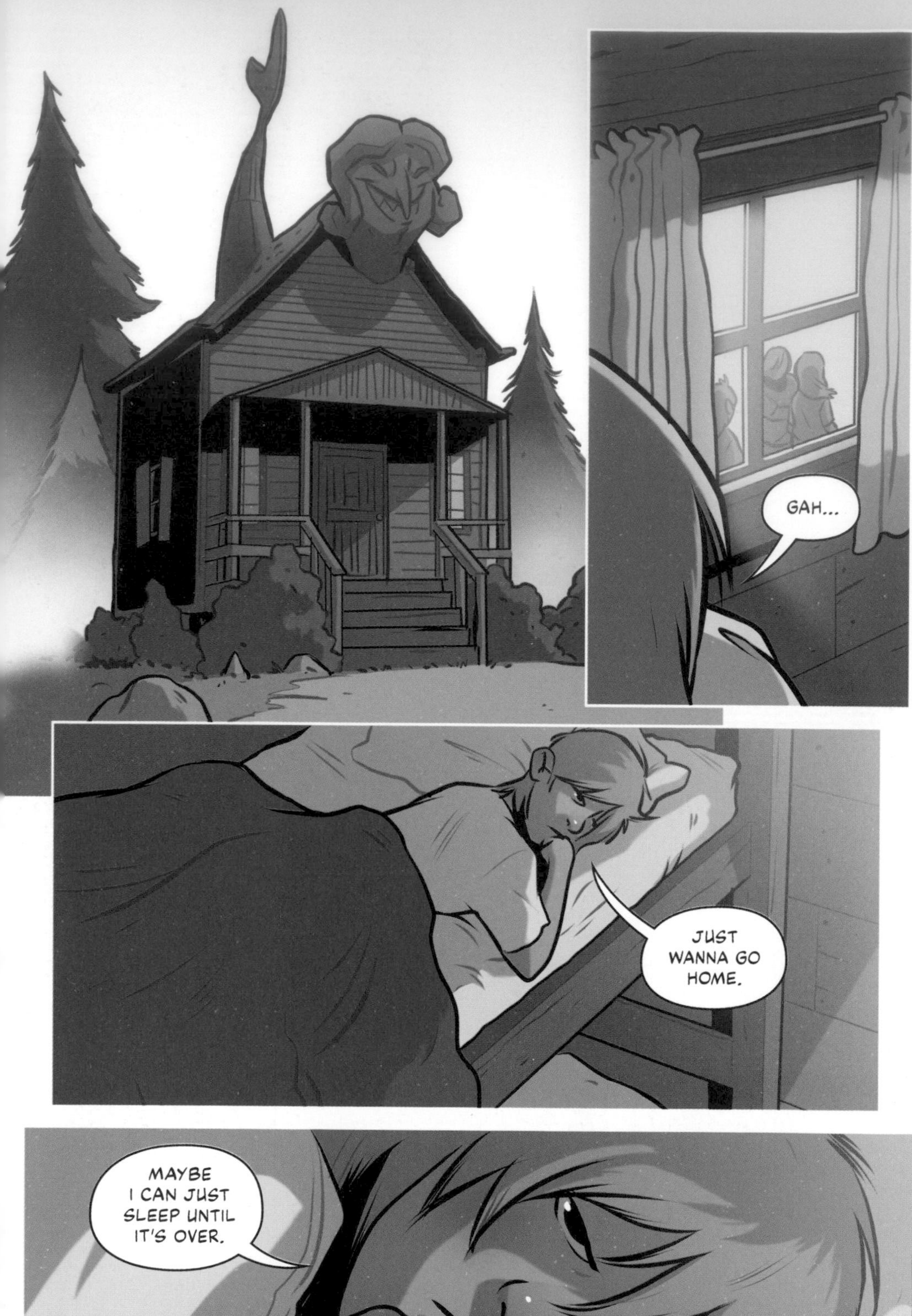

GAH...

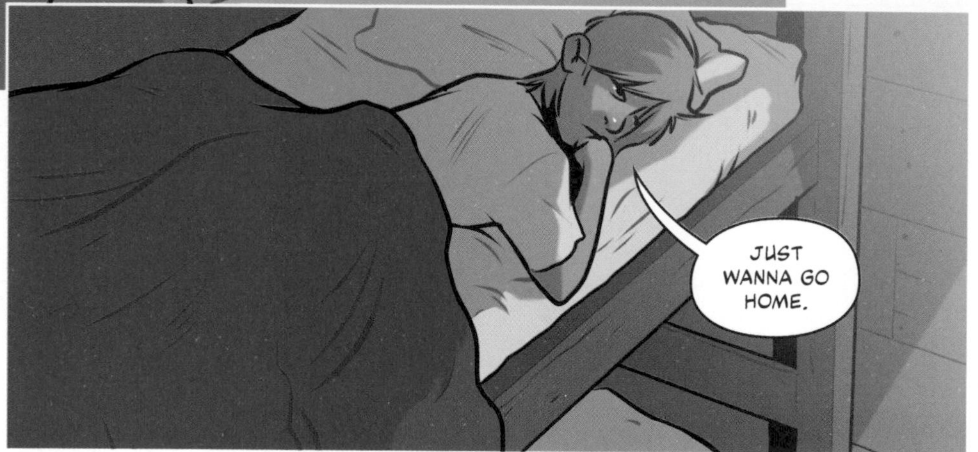

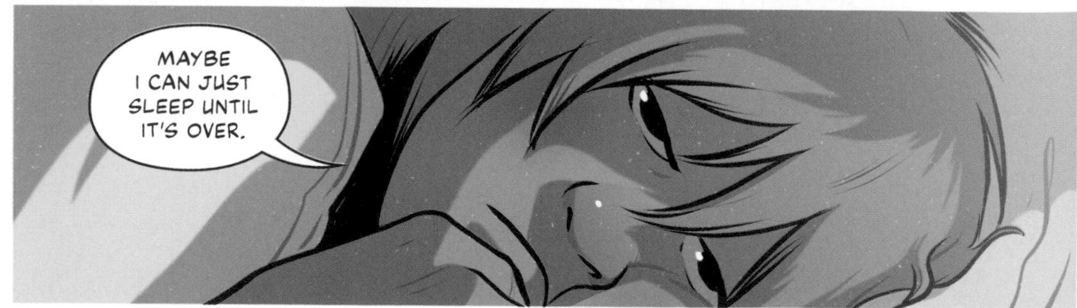

MAYBE I CAN JUST SLEEP UNTIL IT'S OVER.

THUD
THUMP
BUMP
BUMP
SCRITCH
SCRATCH

WHA...
THUMP
BUMP
THUMP
BOOM
THUMP
BUMP

THERE YOU ARE! HAVE YOU BEEN HIDING IN HERE ALL DAY?
IT'S ALMOST FOUR-THIRTY, WIL.
YOU'RE MISSING ALL THE FUN.

OH. HEY, GUYS.

WHAT ARE, UH...
WHAT'RE YA DOING?
I JUST... THOUGHT I SAW SOMETHING.

IT WAS UNDERNEATH HERE.
I THINK THERE WAS A **BEAR** IN HERE.
A BEAR? UNDER THE BED?
LET'S GO GRAB SOME DINNER, YOU'RE PROBABLY JUST HUNGRY.
BESIDES, YOU **NEED** TO SEE THE CAMP COOK. EVERYONE'S SAYING SHE'S A VAMPIRE.
SHE **TOTALLY** IS.

WHAT?
OH... YEAH. LUNCH. SOUNDS GOOD.

YOU MEAN DINNER, WIL. YOU **MISSED** LUNCH.
ARE YOU OKAY?

I GUESS I MUST HAVE BEEN DREAMING, OR SOMETHING.
WAIT, DID YOU SAY THE COOK IS A **VAMPIRE?**

WILLOW, THIS IS RAND, AND THOSE ARE THE STUMP TWINS.
JUST STUMP TWINS, NO FIRST NAMES?
UH...THEY ONLY ANSWER TO THEIR LAST NAME. IT'S REALLY CONFUSING SINCE THEY ALWAYS BOTH ANSWER.
WE MET ON THE... BOAT.
UH...SORRY ABOUT THESE TWO. THEY EAT LIKE PIGS.
MOO
GROSS.
GROSS.
SO GROSS.

DO YOUR HEARING AIDS GIVE YOU SUPER-HUMAN HEARING?
GOOD QUESTION, BRO.
UH...NOPE. JUST NORMAL HEARING.
SORRY.
STOP BEING RUDE, YOU TWO.
THUD
WHOA, BRO!
NO, IT'S FINE. I DON'T MIND ANSWERING QUESTIONS.
I LOST SOME OF MY HEARING WHEN I WAS SIX AFTER I GOT REALLY SICK.
BUT I CAN HEAR JUST FINE NOW, AS LONG AS I HAVE MY EARS ON--I MEAN, MY HEARING AIDS.

DO YOU THINK MAYBE YOU COULD TEACH **ME** SOME SIGN LANGUAGE?

SURE, I GUESS.
HERE'S YOUR FIRST LESSON.
TAP

WHAT DOES IT MEAN?
VAMPIRE. LIKE, OUR CAMP COOK IS FOR REAL A **VAMPIRE**.

DERE'S MORE FOODS, CHILDREN.
WHO VANTS MORE OF DA FOODS?

SHE **IS** REALLY PALE.

AND CHECK OUT THE LIST OF FOOD THAT ISN'T ALLOWED IN CAMP.

Moo

SHE'S NOT EVEN **TRYING** TO HIDE IT, IS SHE?

PLEASES NO RUNNING WHILE FOOD EATING FOR CHILDRENS.

NOT ALLOWED

PEANUTS

GARLIC

CATS

YOU GUYS ARE **MEAN.** SHE'S JUST A WEIRD OLD LADY.
THIS ENTIRE PLACE IS WEIRD.
EARLIER, WHEN I WAS...UH, SLEEPING, I'M SURE I SAW A HUGE, HAIRY...

A HUGE HAIRY WHAT?

PICTURE OF YOUR MOM.

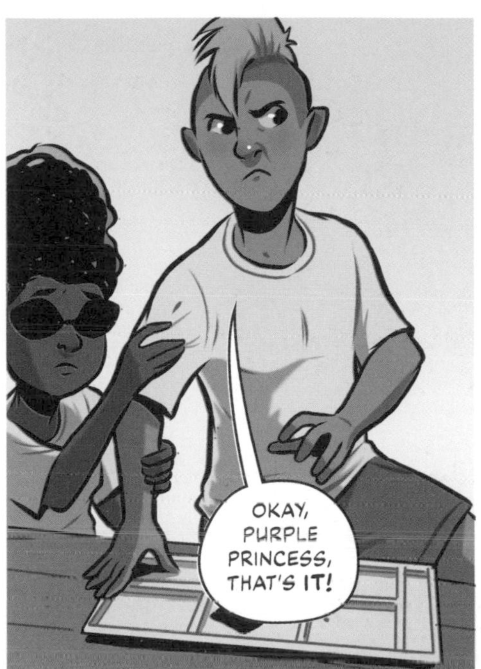
OKAY, PURPLE PRINCESS, THAT'S **IT!**

HEY! **LESS** TALKING, **MORE** EATING.
YOU WON'T WANT TO MISS TONIGHT'S CAMPFIRE ENTERTAINMENT, I **ASSURE** YOU.

AND I'LL BE SPEAKING **EXTRA** LOUD, SO OUR DEAF CAMPER CAN HEAR ME BETTER.

DID TOOTER KILL HER AND TAKE HER JOB?

YEP, AND THEN HE **ATE** HER.

HE **ATE** HER?

YOU GUYS...?

DID HE REALLY **EAT** HER?

AS THE NEWLY APPOINTED CAMP DIRECTOR, IT IS MY **OBLIGATION** TO WELCOME YOU TO CAMP... WHATEVER.
AS MANY OF YOU MAY HAVE GUESSED, I AM IN FACT **THE** CLARENCE TOOTER, WORLD-RENOWNED BIGFOOT HUNTER AND RECIPIENT OF THE **PRESTIGIOUS** THREE-STAR HUNTERS GUILD AWARD.
YOU WILL ADDRESS ME AS MR. TOOTER.
NOW, WHILE **SOME** OF YOU MAY'VE HEARD THE RUMORS THAT THIS ISLAND MIGHT BE HOME TO THE LEGENDARY BIGFOOT, LET ME ASSURE YOU NOW, YOU HAVE **NOTHING** TO FEAR.
SHOULD THE **VICIOUS** BEAST SHOW ITS FACE ANYWHERE NEAR THIS CAMP, I'M FULLY PREPARED TO PROTECT **MY** INTERESTS.
THAT SAID, I HAVE A FEW ANNOUNCEMENTS TO GET TO.
FIRST AND **MOST** IMPORTANTLY, STAY WITHIN THE BOUNDARIES OF THE CAMP, ESPECIALLY AFTER NIGHTFALL.
THE FOG IS INCREDIBLY, ALMOST UNNATURALLY THICK ON THIS ISLAND, AND WE WOULDN'T WANT YOU GETTING LOST, FOR LEGAL REASONS.

NEXT, THE CAMP'S GROUNDSKEEPER, MR. ELRIC, HAS REQUESTED TO BE LEFT ALONE, UNLESS ABSOLUTELY NECESSARY.
THAT'S **FINE** WITH ME, AS I FIND HIM TO BE VERY OFF-PUTTING AND CREEPY.

I FEEL THE **SAME** WAY ABOUT TOOTER.
NO DOUBT.
CHECK IT OUT, WILLOW. IT'S THAT WEIRD, CREEPY GUY AGAIN.

WHO IS THAT?
THAT'S MR. ELRIC.

THAT'S ELRIC?
I MEAN, HE'S KINDA STRANGE, BUT HE COULD HAVE GOTTEN US IN TROUBLE, AND HE DIDN'T?
HE'S SEEMS KINDA OKAY TO ME.

LASTLY, CAMP... WHATEVER IS **PROUD** TO ANNOUNCE ITS VERY **FIRST** DEAF CAMPER.

WILLOW, PLEASE STAND UP FOR US?

THERE SHE IS!

NOW EVERYONE BE SURE TO SPEAK **LOUDER** SO SHE CAN HEAR YOU BETTER.

IT'S **ALSO** THE FIRST TIME THERE'S BEEN A CAMP DIRECTOR WHO COULD BUILD A DAM WITH HIS OWN **TEETH.**
HA
HA
HA
HA
HA
HA
HA

I JUST MEAN, THE WAY HE PUTS THEM ON DISPLAY...
HE MUST **WANT** EVERYONE TO NOTICE.
MAN...I BET HE CAN GNAW THROUGH AN OLD TREE STUMP IN RECORD TIME.

EXCUSE ME, SON?

I'D LIKE TO SPEAK TO YOU IN MY OFFICE.

NOW!

CALLIE, WHY DON'T YOU AND THE OTHER COUNSELORS ENTERTAIN THE CAMPERS WHILE I DEAL WITH THIS.

YOU OKAY?
I **HATE** IT WHEN PEOPLE DO THAT. I JUST WANNA BE TREATED LIKE EVERYONE ELSE.

IT'S NOT YOU, WIL. HE'S JUST A **HUGE** JERK.

WOO-HOO!
OKAY, CAMPERS, WE'RE GONNA HAVE A **SINGIN'** AND A **DANCIN'** PARTY!

MAYBE THAT KURT KID IS COOLER THAN I THOUGHT.

UH...BECAUSE OF **HIM** WE'RE HAVING A DANCE PARTY.
SO... NO.
NOT COOL.

CHOO-CHI CHOO-CHI BOO-CHI
CHOO-CHI BOO-CHI CHOO-CHI
BOO-CHI BOO-CHI BOO-CHI
NO S'MORES UNTIL EVERYBODY DOES THE CHOO-CHI-BOO-CHI!
WELL, THERE'S GONNA BE A LOT OF LEFTOVER S'MORES.
FOR REALS.

LATER
NOW, WHO WANTS TO HEAR THE **BORING** OLD LEGEND ABOUT THIS ISLAND...
AND WHO WANTS TO HEAR ABOUT THE **THRILLING, SPINE-TINGLING** ADVENTURES OF A THREE-STAR HUNTERS GUILD MEMBER WHO HAS TRAVELLED TO THE MOST **DANGEROUS** PLACES ON EARTH?

WHAT SAY YOU?

THE ISLAND!
WE WANNA HEAR THE LEGEND!
THE **LEGEND!**

OH...YOU CHILDREN ARE INSUFFERABLE.
YOU'D PREFER A DUSTY OLD STORY ABOUT THE FOUNDING OF THIS ISLAND RATHER THAN...
YES!

SO BE IT.
BUT IF I **HAVE** TO TELL IT, THEN YOU'RE GOING TO HEAR THE **REAL** STORY, NOT THE WATERED-DOWN, SAFE-FOR-KID-EARS VERSION.

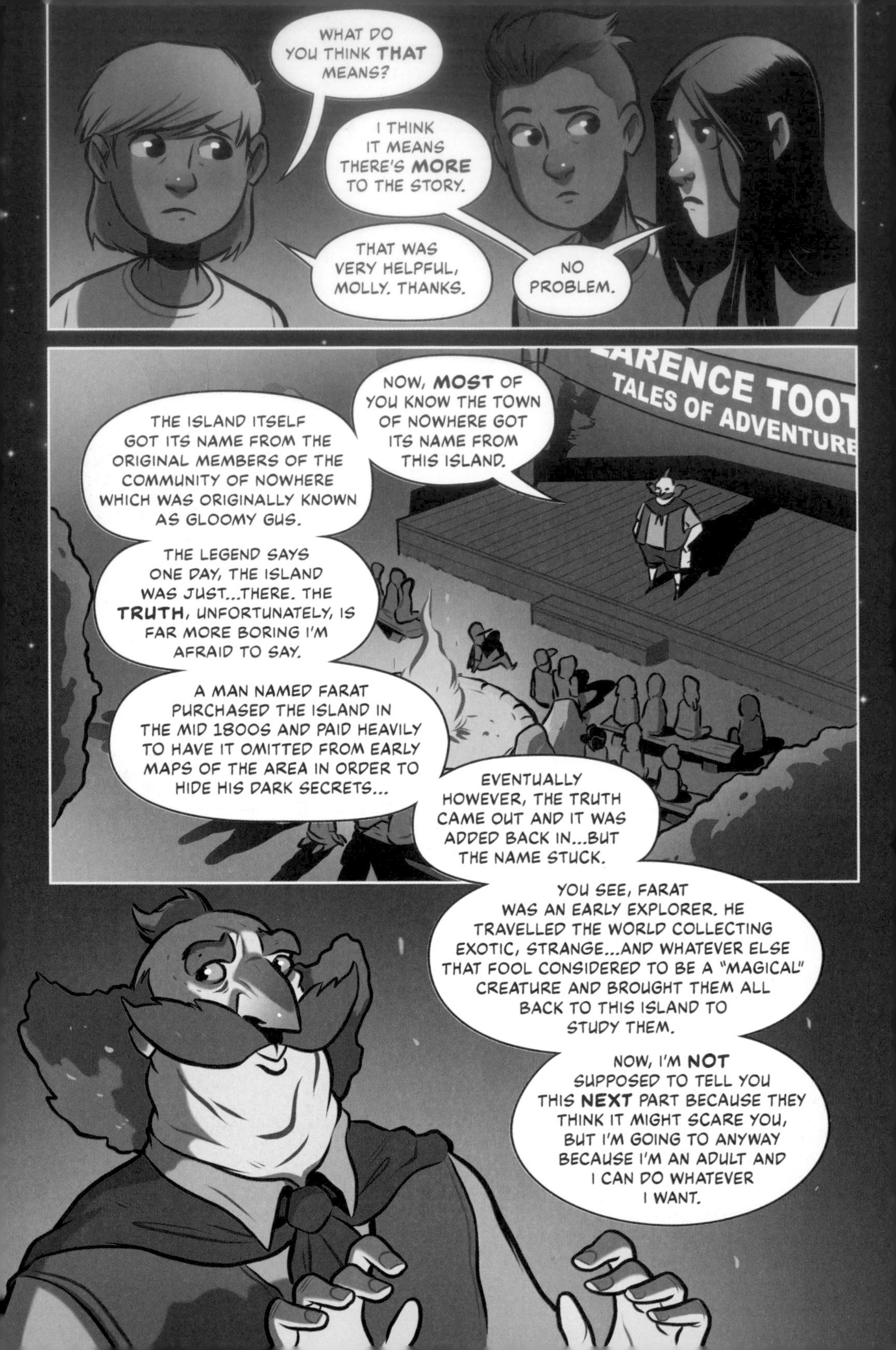

WHAT DO YOU THINK **THAT** MEANS?
I THINK IT MEANS THERE'S **MORE** TO THE STORY.
THAT WAS VERY HELPFUL, MOLLY. THANKS.
NO PROBLEM.
...ARENCE TOOT
TALES OF ADVENTURE...
NOW, **MOST** OF YOU KNOW THE TOWN OF NOWHERE GOT ITS NAME FROM THIS ISLAND.
THE ISLAND ITSELF GOT ITS NAME FROM THE ORIGINAL MEMBERS OF THE COMMUNITY OF NOWHERE WHICH WAS ORIGINALLY KNOWN AS GLOOMY GUS.
THE LEGEND SAYS ONE DAY, THE ISLAND WAS JUST...THERE. THE **TRUTH**, UNFORTUNATELY, IS FAR MORE BORING I'M AFRAID TO SAY.
A MAN NAMED FARAT PURCHASED THE ISLAND IN THE MID 1800S AND PAID HEAVILY TO HAVE IT OMITTED FROM EARLY MAPS OF THE AREA IN ORDER TO HIDE HIS DARK SECRETS...
EVENTUALLY HOWEVER, THE TRUTH CAME OUT AND IT WAS ADDED BACK IN...BUT THE NAME STUCK.
YOU SEE, FARAT WAS AN EARLY EXPLORER. HE TRAVELLED THE WORLD COLLECTING EXOTIC, STRANGE...AND WHATEVER ELSE THAT FOOL CONSIDERED TO BE A "MAGICAL" CREATURE AND BROUGHT THEM ALL BACK TO THIS ISLAND TO STUDY THEM.
NOW, I'M **NOT** SUPPOSED TO TELL YOU THIS **NEXT** PART BECAUSE THEY THINK IT MIGHT SCARE YOU, BUT I'M GOING TO ANYWAY BECAUSE I'M AN ADULT AND I CAN DO WHATEVER I WANT.

THE LEGEND **ALSO** SAYS THAT ONE DAY, THOSE **SAME** CREATURES TURNED ON THEIR MASTER, DESTROYING HIM AND STEALING HIS CHILD, PROBABLY FOR SOME RITUAL.

BEFORE FARAT DIED, HOWEVER, HE SWORE HE'D RETURN ONE DAY TO GET HIS REVENGE.

RIGHT BEFORE HE EXPLODED, OR SO THE STORY GOES, HE SPOKE THESE WORDS... "WHEN THE BLOOD OF MY BLOOD IS SPILLED FROM A STAR, AND THE SHADOWS OF ELVES RETURN FROM AFAR, I WILL ONCE AGAIN WALK THIS PLANE BRINGING DEATH IN TOW."

SO, I GUESS LET'S ALL TRY TO KEEP FROM SPILLING **BLOOD** FROM ANYTHING STAR-SHAPED. YES?

IT'S ALL JUST A BUNCH OF **HOOEY** DESIGNED TO SELL TRINKETS TO GULLIBLE TOURISTS, IF YOU ASK ME.

CLARENCE TOOTER!
I HARDLY THINK THIS IS APPROPRIATE FOR YOUNG EARS!

I MET A GUY ON THE WAY HERE THAT WAS TALKING ABOUT THIS...
ABOUT STARS, I MEAN.
IT'S AMAZING ANYONE WANTS TO COME BACK AFTER HEARING THAT PART.
I'VE BEEN COMING HERE FOR THREE YEARS, AND THAT'S THE FIRST I'VE EVER HEARD OF IT.
YOU GUYS BUYING ANY OF THAT?
I HAVEN'T SEEN ANY MAGICAL CREATURES AROUND HERE. HAVE YOU?

NAH.
HE'S JUST TRYING TO SCARE US BECAUSE WE DIDN'T WANT TO HEAR ABOUT HIS STUFF.

GOOD POINT.

UH... YES.
PERHAPS YOU'RE RIGHT, MISS MIM.
HMPH...
I LIKE HER.
ME TOO.
IT'S TIME FOR BED, MY DEARS..
COUNSELORS, PLEASE SEE YOUR ASSIGNED CAMPERS FIND THEIR WAY TO THEIR CABINS.
CLARENCE TOOT
TALES OF ADVENTURE
SLEEP WELL, CHILDREN. TOMORROW WILL BE FILLED WITH FUN AND GAMES, CRAFTS, AND MANY OTHER WONDERFUL ACTIVITIES.

SNORT
ZZZZZZZZZZ

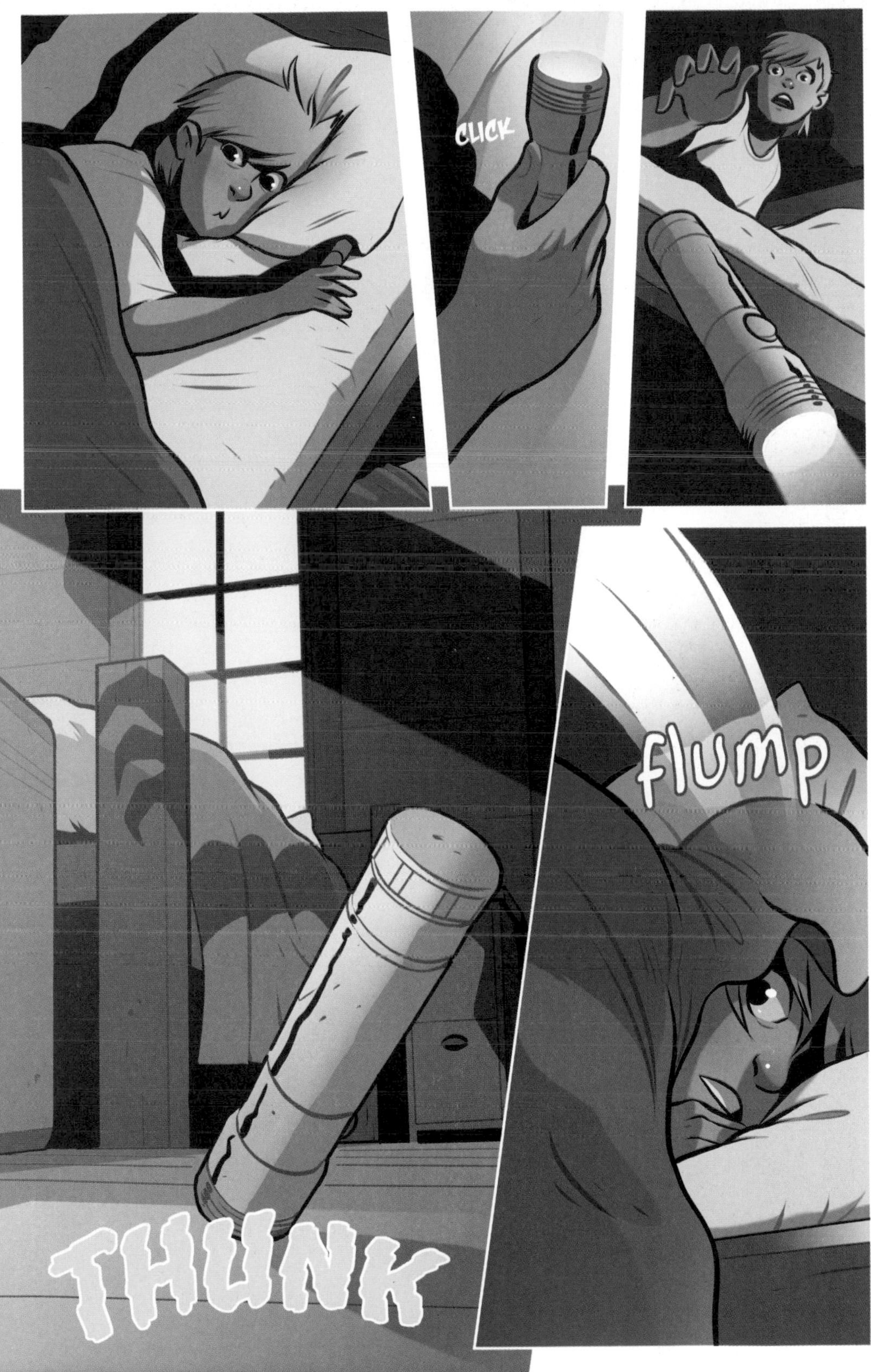
CLICK
THUNK
flump

chicky CHIPS

crinkle

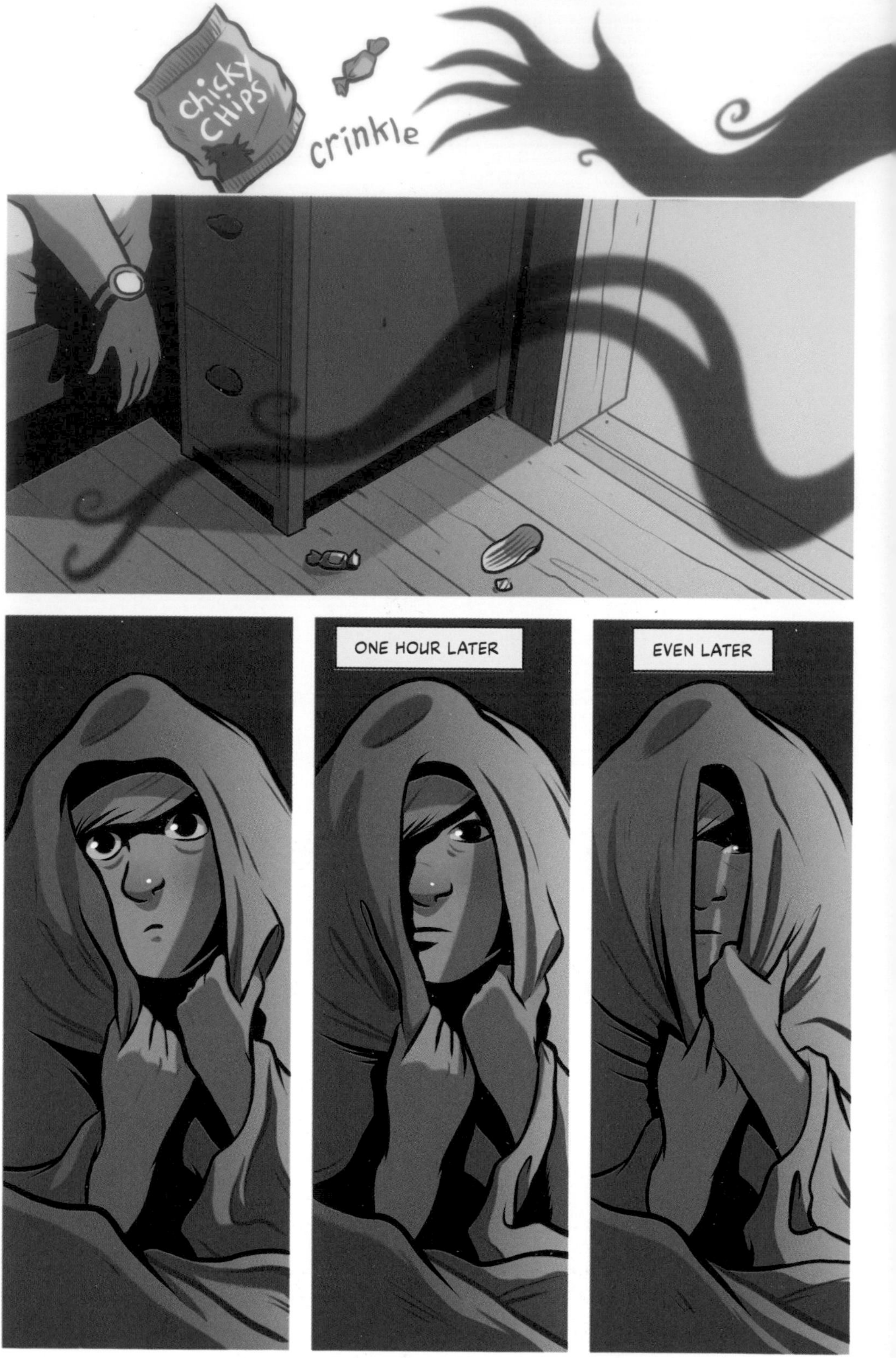

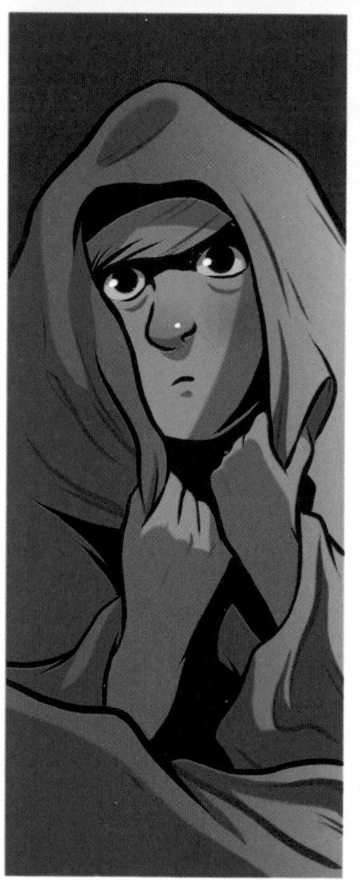

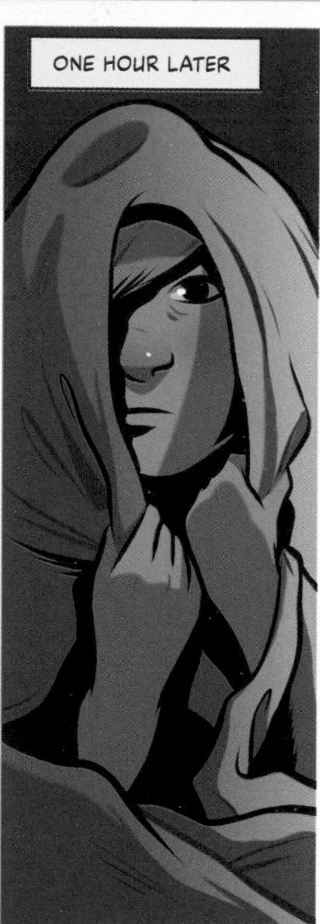
ONE HOUR LATER

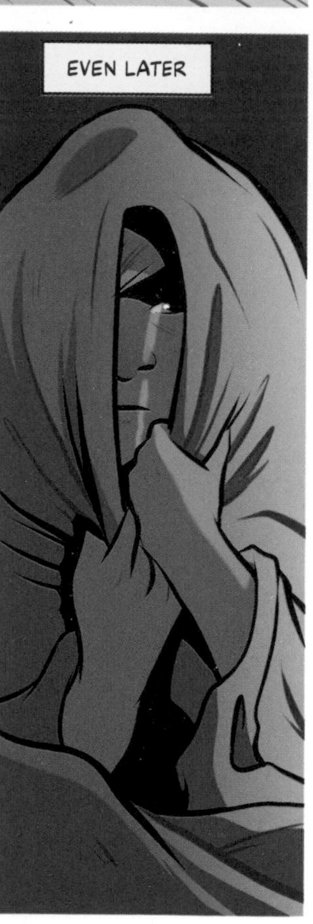
EVEN LATER

WELL, THEY WERE **THERE** WHEN I WENT TO BED!

I **DIDN'T** TAKE YOUR SNACKS, MOLLY.

I DON'T EVEN LIKE CHEESE PIPS.

WELL, **SOMEBODY'S** BEEN GOING THROUGH **MY** BAG **ALSO** BECAUSE MINE ARE GONE, TOO.

click

WHAT'S EVERYONE ALL UPSET ABOUT?

GROSS! WHAT DID I JUST STEP IN?

I WAS WONDERING THAT, AS WELL. WHATEVER IT IS, THERE'S PIECES ALL OVER THE PLACE.

IT'S KINDA SPONGEY.

OKAY, GIRLS, **EVERYONE** OUTSIDE. EMERGENCY CAMP MEETING.
WE'RE GONNA GET TO THE BOTTOM OF THIS RIGHT **NOW**.

I WANT MY CANDY BACK.

LOOKS LIKE **WE** WEREN'T THE **ONLY** ONES.
EVERYBODY PLEASE CALM DOWN.
HEY, HANG BACK A SECOND.
WHAT'S UP, WIL?
SO, LAST NIGHT, I SAW... SOMETHING... IN OUR CABIN.
I WOKE UP... AND SOMEONE, OR SOMETHING, WAS MOVING AROUND BY THE BAGS.
WAS IT THAT BED BEAR?
HILARIOUS.

NO, IT **WASN'T** A BEAR.
SO...WHAT **WAS** IT?
IF I **KNEW** WHAT IT WAS I WOULD **TELL** YOU.
UM... WIL?
I THINK YOU GUYS SHOULD SEE THIS.
WHAT'S UP?
I THINK IT'S MR. ELRIC.

WHAT'S HE DOING?
KINDA LOOKS LIKE HE'S **SIGNING** TO SOMEONE.
CAN YOU READ WHAT HE'S SAYING?

HE **MIGHT** BE SAYING STAY BACK?
I DON'T KNOW. HE'S TOO FAR AWAY.

WHO WOULD HE BE SIGNING **TO?**

GOOD QUESTION.

IT COULD BE THE CAMP NURSE?
MY MOM SAID SHE KNOWS SIGN LANGUAGE.
WHY WOULD THE NURSE BE IN THE WOODS?
SHE ISN'T.
CHECK IT.
MAYBE ELRIC'S JUST TALKING TO THE FOG LEECHES?
STOP IT, MOLLY! FOG LEECHES AREN'T REAL!

BRANG
BRANG
ALANG

BREAKFAST EATING TIME FOR CHILDRENS!
BRANG
WAIT, I THOUGHT VAMPIRES SLEPT DURING THE DAY?
DAYWALKER!
HA!
C'MON, GIRLS! IT'S BREAKFAST EATING TIME FOR CHILDRENS.
HOLD BACK A SEC.
WHAT? WHY?

HEY, EMMA, WOULD YOU AND MOLLY MIND SAVING US A SEAT?
VIOLET AND I ARE GONNA GO SEE WHAT MR. ELRIC IS UP TO.

WE **ARE?**
WHAT IF SOMEONE ASKS **WHERE** YOU ARE?

WHAT IF M...
WHAT IF **MR. TOOTER** NOTICES YOU TWO ARE MISSING?

JUST COVER FOR US.
TELL HIM WE'RE SICK, OR SOMETHING.
WE'LL BE BACK AS SOON AS WE CAN.
I'M STARTING TO **REALLY** FEEL SICK.

WELL...HAVE FUN WITH ALL THAT.
I'MA GO EAT SOME BACON.
BE CAREFUL. THAT GUY'S CREEPY.

AGAIN WITH THE WEIRD GARDEN GNOMES.

I **WISH** THERE WAS A WAY FOR THIS FOG TO BE **THICKER** BECAUSE IT'S NOT **CREEPY** ENOUGH OUT HERE ALREADY.
DO YOU HEAR THAT?
SOUNDS LIKE SOMEONE'S WHISPERING.

THIS IS A **BAD** IDEA, WIL.
LOOK. **MORE** OF THESE STRANGE MARKINGS.
I **WISH** I COULD READ THEM.

WE SHOULD GO BACK.
WHY?
WHY? BECAUSE IF THIS WAS A HORROR MOVIE, THIS IS WHEN THE SCARY MONSTER WOULD JUMP OUT.
YOU WATCH TOO MANY MOVIES, VIOLET.
SALMON?
MUD?
FRUIT COCKTAIL?
WHAT ELSE? AH... GINGERBREAD?
PINECONE?
PRUNES?

IS HE TALKING TO THE GNOMES?
LOOKS LIKE IT.
COME, CHILDREN. THERE'S NO NEED TO BE FRIGHTENED. YOU'RE IN NO DANGER.
WE WERE JUST...I MEAN, WE WERE ONLY...
SNEAKING ABOUT?
UH... YEAH.
SORRY.

IS THERE SOMETHING I CAN ASSIST YOU LADIES WITH ON THIS MORNING?
SOME TEA, PERHAPS?

WHAT... WHAT ARE YOU DOING?

ENDEAVORING TO WAKE THESE POOR SOULS FROM THEIR STONE SLUMBER, IF YOU MUST KNOW.
WAKE UP GARDEN GNOMES?
GARDEN GNOMES? GOOD HEAVENS NO, MY DEAR.
THESE GNOMES ARE VERY MUCH ALIVE.
ONLY, SADLY... THEY'VE TURNED TO STONE.

TURNED TO STONE?

YES. YOU SEE, WHEN A GNOME IS STARTLED, THEY TURN TO STONE AS A DEFENSE MECHANISM.
THE **ONLY** WAY TO FREE THE GNOME FROM ITS STATE OF SLUMBER IS SIMPLY TO **SPEAK** ITS **NAME** OUT LOUD TO THEM.

WHAT ARE THEIR NAMES?

THAT, MY DEAR, IS THE TROUBLE.
GNOMES, YOU SEE, KEEP THEIR NAMES **SECRET**, LEST IT BE USED **AGAINST** THEM IN SOME SPELL.
IT'S NOT AT ALL UNCOMMON FOR GNOMES TO **REMAIN** STONE STATUES UNTIL THE PASSING OF TIME REDUCES THEM TO MERE DUST. THAT IS, OF COURSE, UNLESS BY SOME MIRACLE A PASSERBY HAPPENS TO **KNOW** THEM, OR IS **FORTUNATE** ENOUGH TO SPEAK THEIR NAME BY MERE CHANCE.

I'VE BEEN TRYING TO WAKE THESE LOST GNOMES FOR NEARLY **THIRTY** YEARS WITH NO LUCK, AS YOU CAN SEE.

ONE OF THEM WAS WEARING AN IMPORTANT TALISMAN THAT IS ALSO NOW TRAPPED IN STONE.

I **DESPERATELY** NEED IT RETURNED IF I HOPE TO STOP...

FORGIVE ME. I'M RAMBLING.

THIRTY YEARS?

ALAS, SOME STONE GNOMES DATE BACK MANY HUNDREDS OF YEARS.

IT'S ALL QUITE TRAGIC.

THAT'S SO SAD.

INDEED. BUT NOW, IF YOU HAVE NO FURTHER QUERIES, I SUGGEST YOU REJOIN YOUR FELLOW CAMPERS.
THERE ARE, NO DOUBT, MANY FUN ACTIVITIES PLANNED FOR YOU THIS DAY.

OH... YES.
IT WAS NICE TO MEET YOU, MR. ELRIC.
NICE TO MEET YOU AS WELL, MY DEARS. ON YOUR WAY, NOW.
GOODBYE.
SO, THAT GUY HAS **LOST** HIS **MIND**. WAKING UP GARDEN GNOMES?
HE SEEMED OKAY TO ME.
I THINK HE'S JUST LONELY.
I GUESS, BUT...WAIT. WHAT'S **THAT?**

I DON'T KNOW ABOUT YOU, BUT THIS LOOKS AN AWFUL LOT LIKE A HASTILY BURIED PILE OF MISSING SNACKS TO ME.
BUT...WHY WOULD ANYONE DO THIS?
MAYBE YOU SHOULD ASK THE LONELY GNOME WHISPERER, VI.
I MEAN, YEAH. CLEARLY IT WAS MR. ELRIC, BUT WHY?
WHY GO TO THE TROUBLE TO STEAL IT AND THEN BURY IT?
IT DOESN'T MAKE SENSE.
SO...DON'T FREAK OUT, BUT HE'S STARING RIGHT AT US.

OH JEEZ, LOOK AT THE TIME!
WE'RE LATE FOR THE CRAFTS!
OH NO, NOT THE CRAFTS!!
ARE WE **REALLY** LATE FOR CRAFTS?
I'M NOT EVEN WEARING A WATCH, VIOLET.

WE JUST NEED TO SNEAK IN WITH THE OTHER CAMPERS.
TODAY WE'RE MAKING EVERYONE'S **FAVORITE!!**
EASY PEASY.
SUN-CATCHERS!
YES!
slap

LUNCH TIME
YOU KNOW, THIS CAMP FOOD'S ACTUALLY **REALLY** GOOD.
I **COMPLETELY** AGREE. I WAS ACTUALLY LOOKING FORWARD TO LUNCH.
HEY WIL, TELL THEM WHAT MR. ELRIC WAS DOING WHEN WE FOUND HIM.
YOU GUYS AREN'T GOING TO BELIEVE THIS.
OH YEAH...
THAT DUDE WAS TALKING TO GARDEN GNOMES.
THE LITTLE CONCRETE GUYS?
MOO

YEP, THERE MUST'VE BEEN A DOZEN OF 'EM.
HE'S AN ODD DUDE.
AND YOU FOUND ALL THE MISSING SNACKS?
EVEN MY CHEESE NIPS?
BURIED... IN HIS BACKYARD.
WE COULD TELL TOOTER.
I BET HE WOULD KICK THAT THIEF RIGHT OFF THIS ISLAND.
PASS. I'D RATHER DEAL WITH ELRIC THAN TOOTER.
THAT GUY'S JUST MEAN.
WHATEVS.
snap

SO... **AFTER** CALLIE FALLS ASLEEP, I **NEED** TO SNEAK BACK DOWN THERE.
WHAT? **WHY?**
BECAUSE I PACKED MY **EXTRA** BATTERIES FOR MY HEARING AIDS IN WITH MY SNACKS.
THESE THINGS **ONLY** LAST A **FEW** DAYS, SO I'M GONNA BE IN **TROUBLE** IF I DON'T GET THEM BACK, AND **QUICK.**
I'D SAY THAT'S A **BAD** IDEA--BUT LET'S BE HONEST, **NOBODY'S** SLEEPING MUCH THE WAY CALLIE SNORES ANYWAY, RIGHT?
slurp

NO DOUBT.
HER BREATHING SOUNDS LIKE A BACKED-UP GARBAGE DISPOSAL.

AND WE COME RIGHT BACK? EVEN **IF** WE **DON'T** FIND THE BATTERIES?

GIRLS! DUCK!
SPLAT
DIRECT HIT, BRO.
WHO DID THAT?
WHO DID IT?

POOF
POOF
STUMP TWINS!!
HA
HA
HA
HA
HA
HA
HA
THOSE TWO REALLY KNOW HOW TO BRIGHTEN MY DAY.
I DON'T THINK TOOTER THOUGHT IT WAS FUNNY.
I HEARD HE'S FORCING US TO LISTEN TO MORE OF HIS STUPID BIGFOOT STORIES TONIGHT.
STORY OF MY LIFE.

THEY MIGHT HAVE GONE **TOO** FAR THIS TIME.

THEY **TOTALLY** DID, AND I **LOVE** THEM FOR IT.

GET BACK HERE, YOU LITTLE MONSTERS!

TOOTER JUST TOLD ME HE SENT KURT HOME FOR MOCKING HIM.
HE SAID MY DAD MET HIM AT THE DOCKS LATE LAST NIGHT.

I'LL BET YOUR DAD WASN'T TOO HAPPY ABOUT THAT.

THAT'S JUST IT THOUGH, MY PARENTS DIED WHEN WE WERE YOUNG.
WE LIVE WITH MY AUNT, AND SHE NEVER LEAVES THE HOUSE AFTER DARK.
MAYBE A FAMILY FRIEND PICKED KURT UP INSTEAD?
NO.

TOOTER'S LYING. I COULD SMELL IT ON HIM.

NO OFFENSE, RAND, BUT YOU MIGHT JUST BE SMELLING YOURSELF.

WHO SMELLS?
WHO ARE YOU GUYS TALKING ABOUT?

THAT EVENING
THERE I WAS, CORNERED LIKE SOME KIND OF...THING...IN A CORNER. THE BEAST HAD ME.
AND THEN IT OPENED ITS MOUTH REVEALING ENORMOUS FANGS AND LET OUT A SCREAM LIKE SOME TYPE OF SCREAMING...THING THAT SCREAMS ALL SCARY!
THERE WAS SO. MUCH. DROOL!
I THINK HE'S RUNNING OUT OF WORDS.
SSSSSSS
SSSSS
SSSSSSS
IIIEEEEEEEE!
CRACK
CRACK

WHO DID THAT?
I SAID...

WHO. DID. THAT?

SERIOUSLY, BRO?
NOT COOL.

MY OFFICE, NOW.
IT WASN'T US, BRO.
WE'RE PRETTY SURE WE DIDN'T DO THIS OR THE PUDDING!

OKAY, GIRLS, JUST A REMINDER IN CASE YOU FORGOT.
NO LEAVING THE CABIN AFTER LIGHTS OUT UNLESS IT'S TO USE THE RESTROOM, AND EVEN THEN IT'S ONE AT A TIME.
EVERYONE UNDERSTAND?

MIDNIGHT
GURGLE
SNORT
POSSUMS...
ZZZZZZZZZ

I'M DANCIN' WITH THE POSSUMS, MAMA...
GURGLE
IT'S COLD OUT HERE.
DO WE REALLY HAVE TO DO THIS AT NIGHT?
IT WOULD BE TOO EASY TO SEE US DIGGING UP HIS YARD IN THE DAYTIME.

FINE. BUT LET'S BE QUICK, OKAY?

WE'LL JUST GRAB MY BATTERIES AND COME RIGHT BACK.

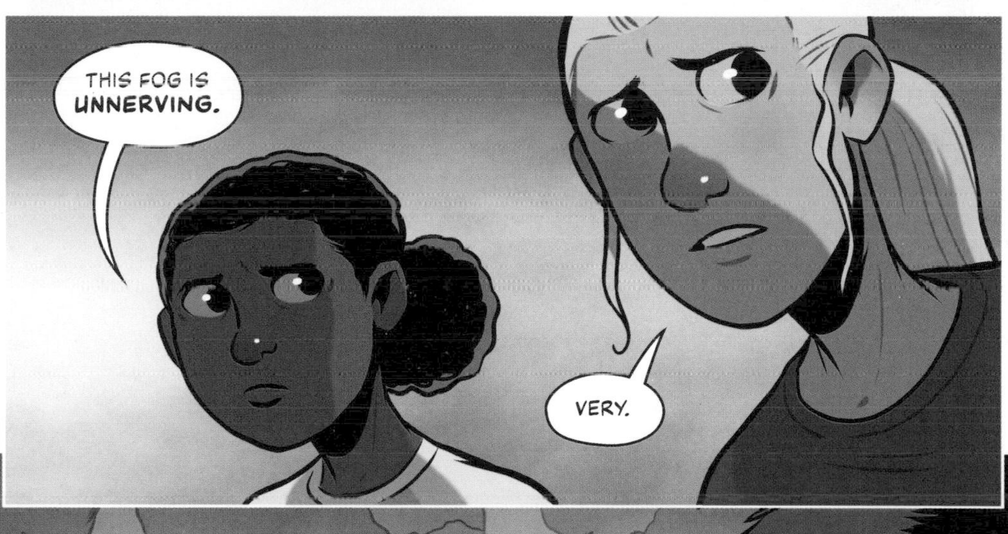
THIS FOG IS **UNNERVING.**
VERY.

IT FEELS LIKE A **MILLION** LITTLE FOG LEECHES ARE **WATCHING** US.
SHUT UP, VIOLET.

THEY'RE RIGHT OVER **HERE**. HELP ME LOOK AROUND.
THERE'S NOTHING HERE, WIL.
THIS **IS** THE **SPOT**, BUT IT'S ALL GONE.
THIS IS... HE MUST HAVE **MOVED** ALL OF IT.
OH WELL, GUESS WE NEED TO GET BACK TO THE CABIN BEFORE CALLIE NOTICES WE SNUCK OUT.
HEY, COME LOOK AT THIS.

WHAT IS IT?

IT'S A MUSHROOM.

GROSS.

LOOKS LIKE THE **SAME** STUFF THAT WAS SCATTERED AROUND IN THE CABINS.

IT'S CALLED ETERNAL SLUMBER.
HOW DO YOU **KNOW** THAT?

THAT'S WEIRD.
WHAT?

I DIDN'T NOTICE THIS EARLIER. ALL OF THE WINDOWS ARE BOARDED UP.
MAYBE HE MOVED AWAY?

SINCE BREAKFAST?

UH...GUYS. LOOK.

IT'S ELRIC.
WHAT'S HE UP TO?

C'MON. LET'S FOLLOW HIM.
FOLLOW HIM? ARE YOU OUT OF YOUR MIND?
LET'S JUST SEE WHERE HE'S GOING. IT WON'T TAKE LONG.

HOW DO YOU KNOW THAT?
HE COULD BE WALKING TO THE OTHER SIDE OF THE ISLAND.

WE ACTUALLY HAVE A SLIGHTLY BIGGER PROBLEM. LOOK.

CALLIE'S AWAKE.
GUESS IT DOESN'T MATTER NOW.
EITHER WAY, WE'RE IN TROUBLE.

WE'VE BEEN WANDERING IN THE WOODS FOR ALMOST AN **HOUR**, WIL.
WE SHOULD HEAD BACK.
I **NEED** TO FIND THOSE BATTERIES.
IF MY HEARING AIDS DIE, I...
CRUNCH
WHAT... WAS THAT?
DON'T LOOK.
WHY?
WHAT IF... WHAT IF IT'S **BONES?**

WHAT THE...?
IS IT BONES?
IT'S... BONES, RIGHT?

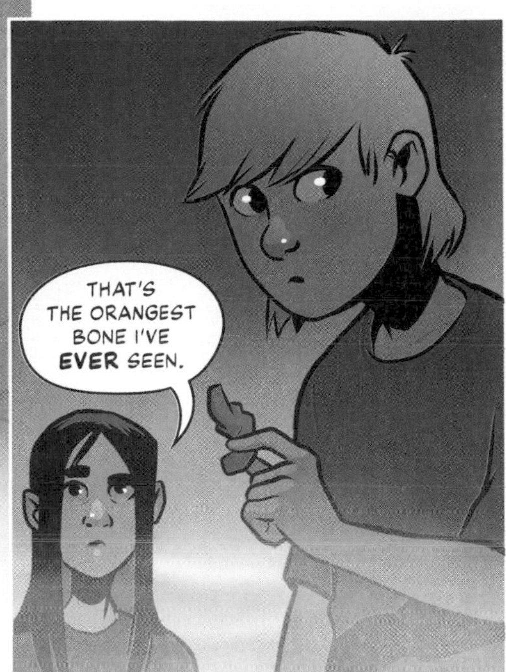
THAT'S THE ORANGEST BONE I'VE **EVER** SEEN.

BUT, WHY WOULD...?
LOOK! I FOUND A POTATO CHIP OVER HERE.

HE MUST BE TAKING THE SNACKS TO HIDE THEM IN THE FOREST.
THAT, **OR** HE'S THROWING A PARTY FOR FOG CLOWNS.
SHUT UP, MOLLY!

THERE'S MORE OVER HERE.

DO YOU GUYS SEE THAT UP AHEAD?
THERE'S A LIGHT.

THAT'S FINE.

YOU GUYS CAN GO BACK IF YOU WANT.

I WANT TO SEE **WHAT** THIS **IS**.

THIS IS CRAZY, WIL.
WHO KNOWS WHO OR WHAT MIGHT BE IN THERE.
I THINK I CAN HEAR SOMETHING UP AHEAD.
SOUNDS ANGRY.
SNORP

HURMPH
BURPH
WAIT, WILLOW.
HOLD ON.

THIS... IS OUR CABIN.

WHAT?
HE LED US IN A CIRCLE.
SO...ELRIC KNEW WE WERE FOLLOWING HIM?
SNORT
ZZZZZZZZZZZZ
CLEARLY.

Z Z Z Z Z Z Z Z Z
CALLIE'S BLOCKING THE ONLY WAY IN.
THERE'S LITERALLY NO ROOM.
WELL, IF WE COULD...SOMEHOW GET PAST HER WITHOUT BEING NOTICED, WE COULD GET IN OUR BEDS AND SHE MIGHT THINK IT WAS ALL JUST A WEIRD DREAM.
SO, WHAT'S THE PLAN?
I THINK I MIGHT HAVE AN IDEA.

GROSS, I JUST PUT MY HAND IN SOMETHING COLD, WET, AND SQUISHY.
ARE YOU SURE THERE'S A DOOR UNDER HERE?
NOPE.

WAIT, I THINK I FOUND IT.
CLICK

creak
SEE? COME ON

HOW DID YOU KNOW ABOUT THIS?

I SAW A GIANT, HAIRY ARM COMING OUT OF IT YESTERDAY.
REMEMBER?

ALL CLEAR.

SHE'S STILL ASLEEP.

Z Z Z Z Z Z Z Z Z

HURRY UP AND BE QUIET.

SNORT
THE POSSUMS... THEY **LOVE** DANCING WITH ME.
GURG
HURP
POSSUMS...

Z Z Z Z Z Z Z Z Z Z Z Z Z Z Z Z
WHY, YES...
SNORP
I WOULD **LOVE** TO DANCE WITH YOU, DUKE OF POSSUMS...

MORNING
HMPH!

GREAT.

JUST GREAT.

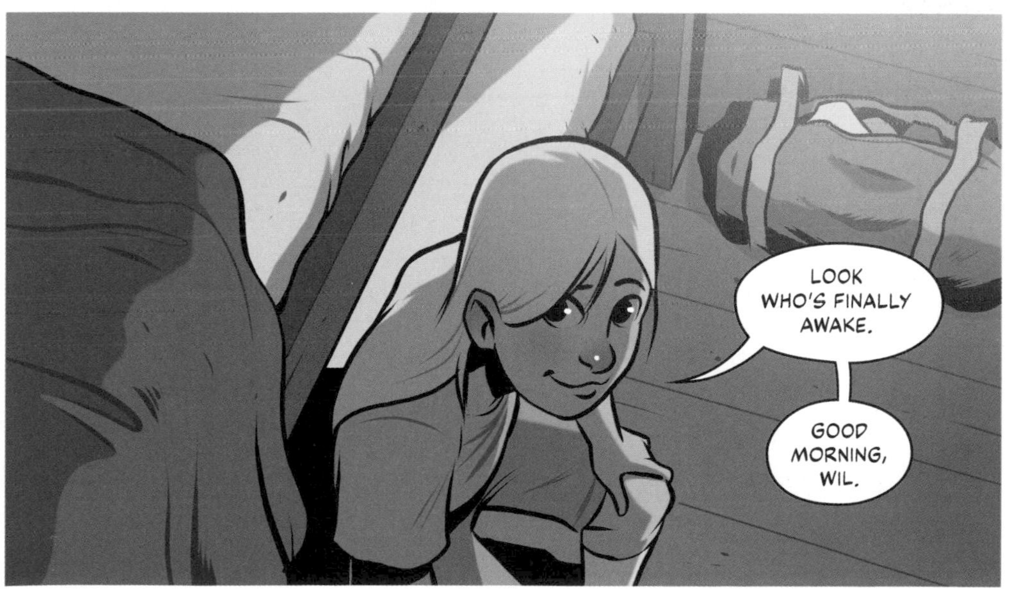
LOOK WHO'S FINALLY AWAKE.
GOOD MORNING, WIL.

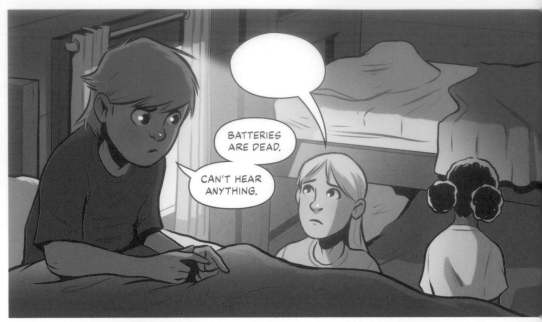

BATTERIES ARE DEAD.

CAN'T HEAR ANYTHING.

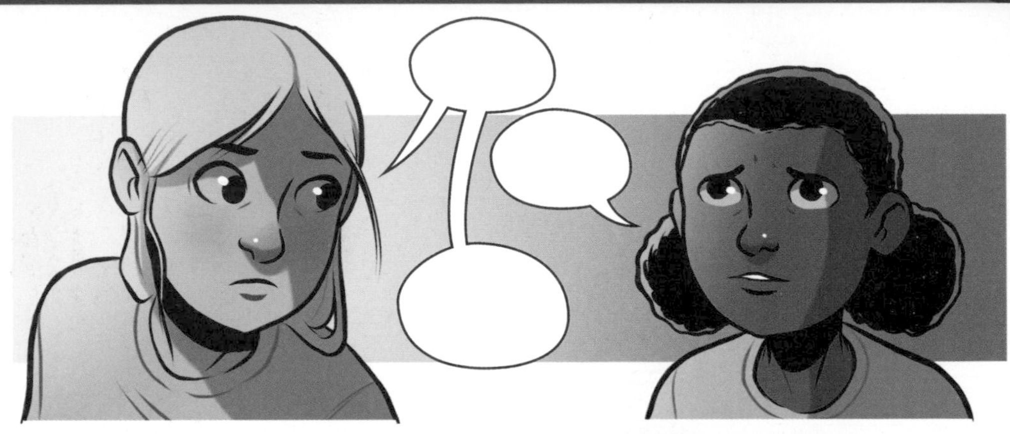

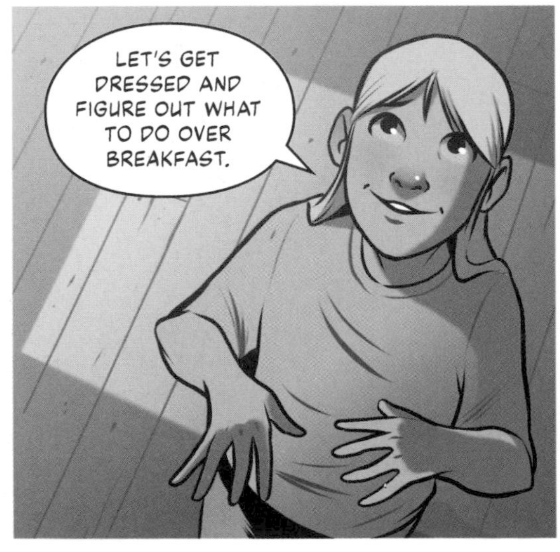

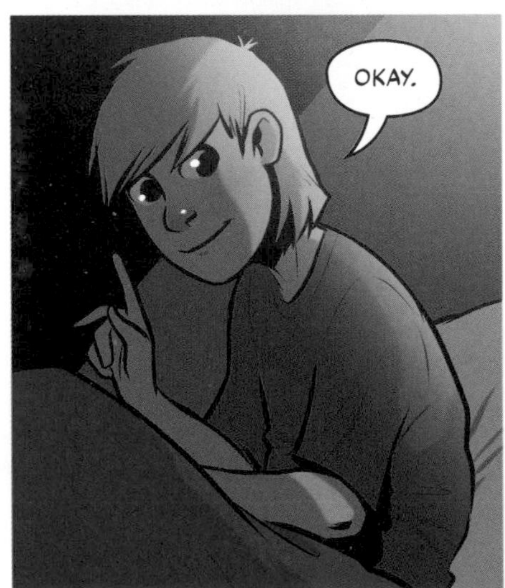

MAYBE WE SHOULD JUST TELL TOOTER? HE MIGHT HELP GET YOUR BATTERIES BACK.

NO, THANKS.

EMMA SAID CALLIE WAS SUPER CONFUSED THIS MORNING WHEN SHE WOKE UP.

HA!

CAN YOU COME WITH ME, PLEASE, DEAR?
HUH?

WHAT FOR?

I HAVE SOMETHING FOR YOU.
CAN I COME, TOO?

OF COURSE.

PLEASE HAVE A SEAT, WON'T YOU.
NOW, I BELIEVE THESE...
...BELONG TO YOU?
THANK YOU.

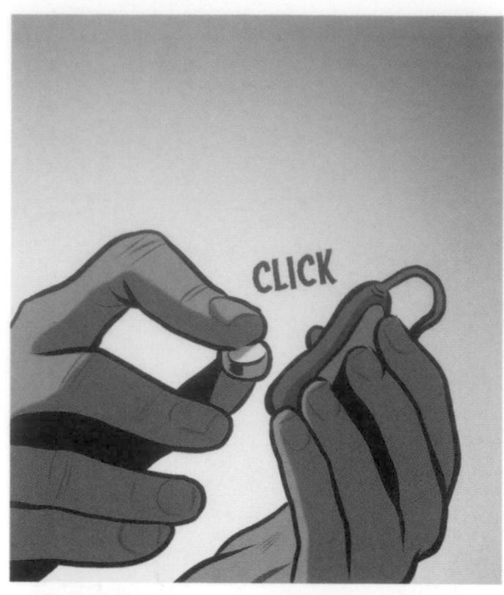
CLICK

BETTER?
SO MUCH.

HOW...I MEAN, WHERE DID YOU **FIND** THESE?

A FRIEND OF MINE **FOUND** THEM AND THOUGHT YOU **MIGHT** BE NEEDING THEM.

A FRIEND?
BANG
KLUNG
BING
KA-CHAK
THUMP

MY GOODNESS, A **MOUSE** MUST HAVE KNOCKED OVER THAT STATUE?
OR PERHAPS IT WAS THE **WIND**... BEHIND THE... CUPBOARD?
TINY EARTHQUAKE?
NO?
NOT BUYING IT?
NOPE.
NOT AFTER **THOSE** EXCUSES, NO.
VERY WELL.
WAKE UP, TOAST! YOU CLUMSY OLD GNOME.

SO...HIS NAME IS TOAST?
YOU NAMED HIM TOAST?

OH HEAVENS, NO. HE NAMED **HIMSELF** THAT.

IT'S... IT'S...A **REAL** GNOME.

NICE TO MEET YOU, MR. TOAST.

NICE TO MEET YOU, TOO, CHILD.

NOW GIRLS, I'M GOING TO NEED YOU TO **SWEAR** TO ME THAT YOU'LL **NOT** SPEAK OF WHAT YOU'VE SEEN HERE TODAY.
NOT EVERYONE IS AS...UNDERSTANDING OF SUCH, UH...THINGS.
WE WOULDN'T WANT POOR TOAST TO BE IN DANGER, NOW WOULD WE?
NO...I MEAN YES. YES, WE CAN KEEP THIS A SECRET.
SO...IF GNOMES ARE **REAL** DOES THAT MEAN...
DOES THAT MEAN THE **REST** OF THE STORIES ARE **TRUE?** DOES IT MEAN THIS ISLAND IS **FILLED** WITH **MANY** OTHER MAGICAL AND MAJESTIC CREATURES **BEYOND** IMAGINATION?
YES.
BUT I MUST CAUTION YOU **NOT** TO GO SEARCHING FOR THEM. MANY OF THEM DON'T WISH TO BE "DISCOVERED" AND CAN GROW QUITE AGGRESSIVE IF THEY ARE SEEN BY HUMANS.
EVEN... UNICORNS?
SAY YES.

UH, WELL, TECHNICALLY UNICORNS ARE...
BOOM BOOM BOOM
CLICK

PARDON ME, NURSE MIM, WOULD YOU BE ABLE TO HELP ME IDENTIFY SOMETHING?
I THINK SOMEONE'S PLAYING GAMES WITH ME.
PROBABLY THE STUMP KIDS.

I KEEP FINDING THESE SCATTERED ALL OVER MY CABIN AND I'M GROWING TIRED OF IT.

AND SPEAKING OF TIRED, WOULD YOU ALSO, BY CHANCE, HAVE ANYTHING FOR FATIGUE?
I'M SO TIRED ALL THE TIME.

SAY, WHAT A SUPERB LOOKING YARD GNOME.

WOULD YOU MIND IF I PUT IT IN MY OFFICE?

OH, I'M AFRAID I'M **QUITE** ATTACHED TO THIS LITTLE GUY.

PERHAPS YOU CAN FIND ANOTHER?

ER...YES, CERTAINLY.

ARE YOU ENJOYING CAMP, WILLOW?

BADOOM
THAT MAN IS A BUFFOON.

A VERY **DANGEROUS** BUFFOON.

NOW, I THINK IT'S TIME FOR YOU GIRLS TO BE ON YOUR WAY. **MIND** WHAT YOU'VE LEARNED TODAY.
YOU ARE NOW THE KEEPERS OF A VERY **SPECIAL** SECRET.
WE WILL.

OUR FRIEND WANTED ME TO PASS ALONG A **MESSAGE** AS WELL.
HE SAID IT'S NOT SAFE TO SNEAK ABOUT AT NIGHT, AS THERE'S NO TELLING **WHO** MIGHT BE WATCHING.
HE SAID YOU WOULD UNDERSTAND?

WONDERFUL. YOU'D BETTER GET BACK OUT THERE. DON'T WANT TO MISS ALL THE FUN AND GAMES.
WE WILL. THANK YOU, NURSE MIM.
THAT WAS A REAL, LIVE GNOME, WIL!
TOAST, I NEED YOU TO TAKE A MESSAGE TO ELRIC.
TOAST!
WAKE UP, TOAST!
YOU LAZY GNOME.

THEY'RE GOING SWIMMING IN THE LAKE.
WE'D BETTER HURRY AND GET CHANGED.
THAT'S A **BIG** PASS FOR ME.
WHAT? **WHY?**

WELL, **FIRST** OF ALL, WHO KNOWS **WHAT'S** LIVING IN THAT LAKE, RIGHT?
AND **SECOND**, I COULD **REALLY** USE A **NAP** AFTER LAST NIGHT'S NATURE WALK. I'M POOPED.

ME TOO. BUT WHAT IF WE GET CAUGHT SKIPPING?
IT'S NOT LIKE THEY'RE GONNA SEND US HOME, VI. RELAX.

DINNER
SERIOUSLY? THAT'S LIKE THE **ONLY** THING SHE WAS LOOKING FORWARD TO.
WE WEREN'T IN THE WATER TWO MINUTES BEFORE IT HAPPENED.

DO YOU HAVE **ANY** IDEA WHAT DID THE BITING?

NO, BUT NURSE MIM SAID SHE'D BE FINE.
SHE GAVE HER SOME MEDS FOR THE PAIN AND THEY'VE MADE HER **HILARIOUSLY** DROWSY.

WHADEVS, SMOLLY... I'S FINE.
SO, WHAT **ELSE** DID WE MISS?
I HEARD TOOTER SENT KURT HOME.

DAY SEMPT HIM **HOME?**
AW YOU SEWIUSH?

THAT'S WHAT LILY SAID.
BESIDES, WHO CARES? HE WAS A JERK.
BUT ALL HE DID WAS MAKE FUN OF TOOTER.
THE STUMP TWINS ATTACKED HIM WITH **PUDDING** AND **FIRECRACKERS**, AND THEY'RE **STILL** HERE.

WELL, THAT'S BECAUSE THEIR **DAD** IS THE PRESIDENT OF THE TOURISM BOARD THAT HIRED MM... MR. TOOTER.
HOW DO YOU KNOW THAT?
I'M AWESOME?

WHERE WERE YOU TWO ALL AFTERNOON?
TAKING NAPS.
WE COULD USE ONE OF THOSE.

WE WERE ALSO MAKING PLANS FOR TONIGHT.
PLANS? PLANS FOR **WHAT?**
DON'T YOU HAVE SOME PUDDING TO THROW, OR SOMETHING?
WHATEVER.
QUICK THINKING, MOLLY.
WE'RE GOING BACK DOWN TO THE WOODS TONIGHT, AFTER CALLIE FALLS ASLEEP.

WE ARE?
I THOUGHT ELRIC FOUND AND RETURNED YOUR BATTERIES?

HE **DID**, EMMA. BUT LOOK, ELRIC IS UP TO **SOMETHING,** AND I WANT TO KNOW WHAT IT IS.
HE'S TRYING TO COVER HIS TRACKS BY RETURNING MY BATTERIES.

BUT, WHAT ABOUT HIS WARNING NOT TO BE OUT AGAIN AFTER DARK?
RIGHT? WHAT'S HE HIDING?

DON'T YOU GUYS WANT TO FIND OUT?
NOPE.

WE GOT LUCKY LAST NIGHT, WIL.
WHAT IF WE GET CAUGHT THIS TIME? WHAT IF THEY SEND US HOME?
I DON'T WANT TO BE SENT HOME.
NOBODY'S GETTING SENT HOME.
WHEN WE FIND WHAT ELRIC IS UP TO, WE'LL TELL TOOTER... OR WHOEVER. I'M SURE THEY'LL BE HAPPY WE DID WHAT WE DID.
SOUNDS RISKY TO ME.
TRUST ME. I'VE GOT IT ALL FIGURED OUT.
THERE WON'T BE ANY SURPRISES THIS TIME. RIGHT, VIOLET?
UH... YES!
I MEAN, NO. NO SURPRISES SUCH AS GNOMES AND UNICORNS!
I MEAN, NONE OF THOSE THINGS FOR SURE... BECAUSE THOSE AREN'T REAL THINGS AND I'M GONNA STOP TALKING NOW.

Z Z Z Z Z Z

MAYBE THEY SHOULD CHANGE THE NAME OF THIS PLACE TO CAMP SUPER CREEPY FOG.

RIGHT? I CAN **BARELY** SEE MY OWN **FEET.**

BE AS QUIET AS YOU CAN UNTIL WE REACH THE WOODS.

WE **DON'T** WANT TO WAKE UP MR. ELRIC.

OH...THAT'S JUST MY **HEART** BEATING ITS WAY OUT OF MY CHEST.

NO...IT SOUNDS LIKE FOOTSTEPS.
COMING THIS WAY.
HIDE.

IT'S PRETTY SPOOKYFRUITS OUT HERE, GUYS.
MAYBE WE SHOULD GO BACK?

I DON'T SEE THE GIRLS, ANYWAY.

IT'S THE BOYS.

WHAT ARE YOU DOING HERE?
WHAT ARE YOU DOING HERE?
IT'S NONE OF YOUR BUSINESS.
YEAH...WELL... MAYBE WE JUST WANTED TO MAKE SURE YOU GUYS WEREN'T IN DANGER?
IS THAT WHY YOU BOYS ARE FOLLOWING US?
BECAUSE WE'RE HELPLESS GIRLS WHO CAN'T TAKE CARE OF OURSELVES?
NO... I MEAN, OF COURSE NOT.
WE JUST...
WE JUST... I THOUGHT YOU MIGHT HAVE BEEN... MY BROTHER.
IT'S STUPID.

SWOOOSH
TCHRRK
AHH!!!

AHHH!
SWISSHHH
FWOOSH
STOP!
STAY BACK!

RROARRR
slap
PUNT

UH...
HEY, I'M GONNA JUST LAY DOWNS FERS SMECKIN...
RUN!

FOLLOW ME! I KNOW THE WAY BACK AND--

CRANCH

SWOOOSH

GET AWAY!

RABIES!

PUNCH
I SAID PUT ME DOWN!

flump

WILLOW!
ARE YOU OKAY?
WE'RE ALL GONNA NEED RABIES SHOTS, YOU GUYS.

WHAT ARE THESE THINGS?
NO IDEA.
WELL, I HOPE THEY LIKE BEING HIT WITH ROCKS.
VIOLET, **STOP**. WHAT ARE YOU DOING?
DON'T WORRY. I'M A GREAT SHOT.

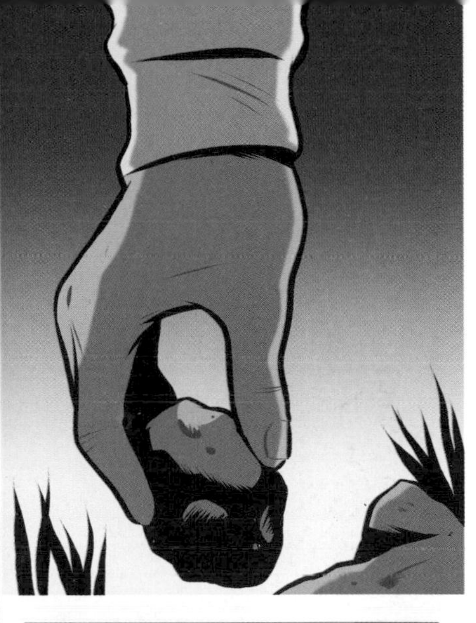

LOOK RIGHT HERE AT THIS ROCK AND SAY CHEESE, YOU FOUL LITTLE--

IT'S VERY ILL-ADVISED TO HARM OR ANGER THE CHICKCHARNEES, GIRL.

TO DO SO IS TO INVITE GREAT MISFORTUNE UPON YOURSELF AND LOVED ONES.

BE GONE WITH YOU! LEAVE THESE CHILDREN ALONE.
THEY MEANT NO TRESPASS.
NOW, IF EVERYONE WILL **CALM** THEMSELVES, I BELIEVE INTRODUCTIONS ARE IN ORDER.

CHILDREN, THIS GENTLE BEAST WHO HAS COME TO YOUR AID IS THATCH, BUT YOU WILL KNOW HIM BY HIS MORE COMMON NAME...
BIGFOOT.
NO WAY.

I RAISED HIM MYSELF, AS HE WAS MERELY A CHILD WHEN HIS PARENTS WERE... WELL, AFTER HIS PARENTS DIED.
AMAZING.
I ASSURE YOU THAT YOU'RE IN NO DANGER FROM HIM--THAT IS, AS LONG AS YOU DON'T MIND HIM EATING **ONE** OF YOU FOR SUPPER.

A FUNNY!

I'M JUST MAKING A **FUNNY**, CHILDREN.

THATCH IS A VEGETARIAN.

YOU KNOW, FOR KIDS WILLING TO STROLL AROUND A DARK FOREST AT NIGHT, BLANKETED IN DENSE FOG AND **SURROUNDED** BY UNSEEN DANGERS, YOU SURE ARE A JUMPY BUNCH.

COME WITH ME, AND I'LL SEE TO YOUR INJURIES.

ELRIC'S CABIN

...OF COURSE I'M NOT AS WELL-VERSED AS SOMEONE SUCH AS YOURSELF, MY DEAR.

BUT I'VE DONE MY BEST OVER THE YEARS IN ORDER TO BETTER COMMUNICATE WITH HIM.

AH...THERE WE ARE, ALL BANDAGED UP. THIS OINTMENT HAS... SPECIAL HEALING QUALITIES AND SHOULD HAVE YOU BACK TO NORMAL IN A DAY, OR SO.

NURSE MIM MAKES IT HERSELF.

WAIT, BACK UP.
YOU TAUGHT HIM...HOW TO SIGN?

PERHAPS YOU'D LIKE TO ASK HIM YOURSELF?

UH... HELLO?

HELLO.

THANK YOU FOR HELPING ME AND MY FRIEND.

MY NAME IS WILLOW.

WUH WOH

THIS IS WHY NURSE MIM KNOWS SIGN LANGUAGE, ISN'T IT?
THIS IS AMAZING.

SO, MR. ELRIC, ARE THESE BOOKS FOR REAL?
MAGIC?
GNOME LORE?
MERMAIDS?
THIS ISLAND IS HOME TO MANY MAGICAL CREATURES. A FEW SHOULD BE AVOIDED AT ALL COSTS, BUT MOST OF THEM ARE FRIENDLY ENOUGH IN THEIR OWN WAY.
NONE OF THEM, HOWEVER, LIKE BEING DISTURBED AND VERY MUCH PREFER TO REMAIN HIDDEN.
IT HAS BEEN MY HONOR AND RESPONSIBILITY TO SEE THAT THEY ARE KEPT SAFE FROM THE OUTSIDE WORLD, AND THAT THE OUTSIDE WORLD IS KEPT SAFE FROM THEM.
DO YOU UNDERSTAND WHAT I'M SAYING?
WE CAN'T TELL ANYONE ABOUT THATCH, OR IT COULD PUT HIM IN DANGER...

PRECISELY.
I FEAR HE WOULD BE IN **GREAT** DANGER IF CERTAIN PARTIES WERE TO BE MADE AWARE OF OUR...
...**HIS** PRESENCE.

YOU'RE TALKING ABOUT MR. TOOTER.

INDEED, I AM. HE IS **FAR** MORE DEVIOUS THAN **ANYONE** KNOWS.

IT WAS NO **MERE** COINCIDENCE THAT LED HIM TO BECOME THIS CAMP'S NEW DIRECTOR. I ADVISED **AGAINST** IT, BUT ALAS, THE PEOPLE IN CHARGE WOULD **NOT** BE SWAYED.

I SUPPOSE I CAN'T BE TOO ANGRY WITH THEM, AS THEY REMAIN FULLY UNAWARE OF THIS ISLAND'S MANY LIVING TREASURES.

NO, CLARENCE TOOTER IS A **CLEVER** MAN. HE IS HERE FOR **ONE** REASON AND ONE REASON **ONLY**. TO HUNT OUR LEGENDARY FRIEND HERE.

I HAVE TO BE HONEST WITH YOU, NOW. I'M EMBARRASSED TO SAY THAT IT WAS I WHO STOLE YOUR SNACKS THAT NIGHT, AS SOME OF YOU HAVE SUSPECTED.
YOU SEE, A CERTAIN HAIRY FRIEND OF MINE LIKES THESE CHIPS AND CANDIES THE CAMPERS BRING EVERY YEAR...

crunch
...DESPITE THE WARNINGS THAT THEY ARE NOT ALLOWED.

AND EVERY YEAR, I DO MY BEST TO KEEP HIM AWAY FROM THE CAMP.
THIS YEAR HOWEVER, WITH MR. TOOTER ABOUT...
I COULDN'T RISK THE TEMPTATION THESE SALTY GOODIES PRESENTED, AND I TOOK IT UPON MYSELF TO SEE THEY WERE REMOVED. I AM...SORRY.

I KNEW IT! I MEAN... YEP.
THAT ACTUALLY MAKES A LOT OF SENSE.

WILLOW, LOOK! **UNICORNS!** I'M IN HEAVEN!

YES, INDEED. PLEASE DO MAKE YOURSELVES AT HOME, MY FRIENDS.

MR. ELRIC...
WHERE DID YOU GET THAT PHOTO?

IT WAS A GIFT FROM MS. CALDEN.
WHY DO YOU ASK, MY DEAR?
BECAUSE WE HAVE THE **SAME** PHOTO ON A SHELF IN OUR DEN.

IT'S FROM WHEN MY DAD WENT HERE AS A KID.
THAT'S **HIM** WITH THE GLASSES STANDING NEXT TO...

IS THAT HAIRY KID...IS THAT THATCH?

IT **IS.**
YOU HAVE A KEEN EYE.

I DON'T UNDERSTAND.

I FELT IT **MIGHT** BE GOOD FOR HIM TO ATTEND CAMP WITH OTHER CHILDREN.
HE WAS PAINFULLY SHY...
HE SPENT ALL OF HIS LIFE UP 'TIL THEN WITH ME, AND I'M SO OLD.
IT DIDN'T WORK OUT AS I HAD HOPED.

WHAT DO YOU MEAN?
SOME OF THE KIDS... THEY WERE CRUEL.
SO, HE SNUCK AWAY ONE NIGHT AND REFUSED TO RETURN.

I TRIED TO DRESS HIM IN A WAY THAT HE MIGHT FIT IN, BUT IN THE END, WELL... KIDS KNOW.
THE FACT THAT NOBODY ELSE SPOKE SIGN LANGUAGE DIDN'T HELP ANYTHING.
EVEN WITH MIM'S HELP.
HE'S THE MISSING CAMPER.
YES.
WUH WOH

BONG
BONG

OH DEAR, THE HOUR HAS GROWN QUITE LATE.
I'M AFRAID I MUST INSIST YOU ALL HEAD BACK TO YOUR CABINS WITHOUT DELAY.
YOU'LL NOT WANT TO MISS OUT ON MORNING ACTIVITIES!

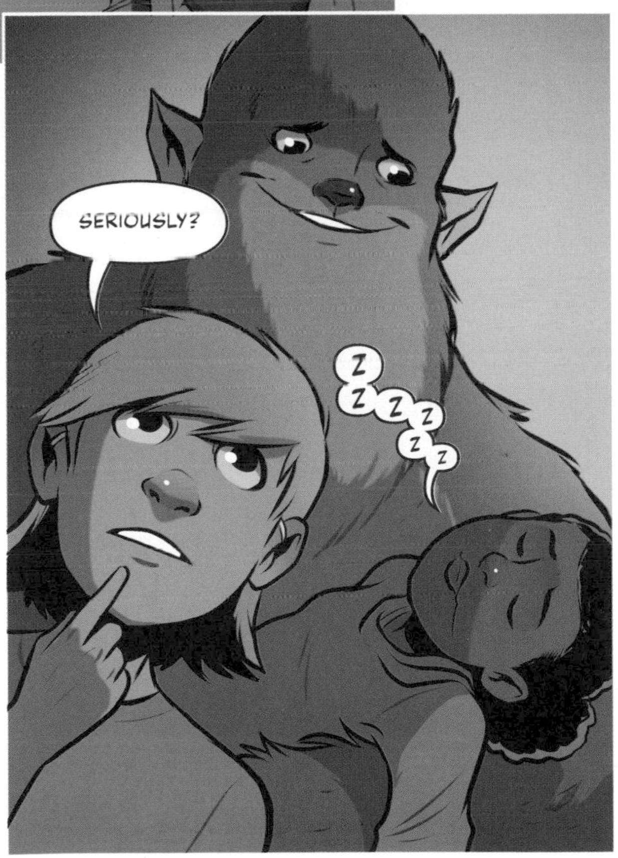
SERIOUSLY?
Z Z Z Z Z Z

I AM PRETTY TIRED, BUT THIS WAS THE BEST NIGHT OF MY LIFE!

GOOD NIGHT, MR. ELRIC.
THANKS FOR THE TEA.
I KNEW TOOTER WAS LYING ABOUT HIS BIGFOOT STORIES.
IS WAS NICE TO MEET YOU, THATCH.
NICE GIRL.
C'MON. WE HAVE A BIG DAY OF MAKING STUPID ARTS AND CRAFTS TOMORROW.
YEAH, OKAY.

HERE, TAKE THIS WITH YOU.
IT'S **MY** JOURNAL. IT HOLDS **MANY** OF THE SECRETS OF THIS ISLAND. I THOUGHT PERHAPS YOU MIGHT FIND IT... ENLIGHTENING.
DON'T YOU NEED IT?
IT'S TIME IT FOUND A NEW HOME, I THINK.
THANK YOU. I PROMISE TO KEEP IT SAFE.
I KNOW YOU WILL.

WHAT?
ONLY THE GIRLS GET GIFTS?
NOT COOL, BRO.
C'MON, YOU TWO. DON'T BE RUDE.

OH, NO, I HAVE SOMETHING VERY SPECIAL FOR YOU BOYS.
COME CLOSER. YOU'LL NOT WANT TO MISS THIS.

NOW, GENTLEMEN, FOR WHAT IT'S WORTH, IT WAS TRULY A PLEASURE MEETING YOU.
NICE TO MEET YOU TOO, ELRIC.

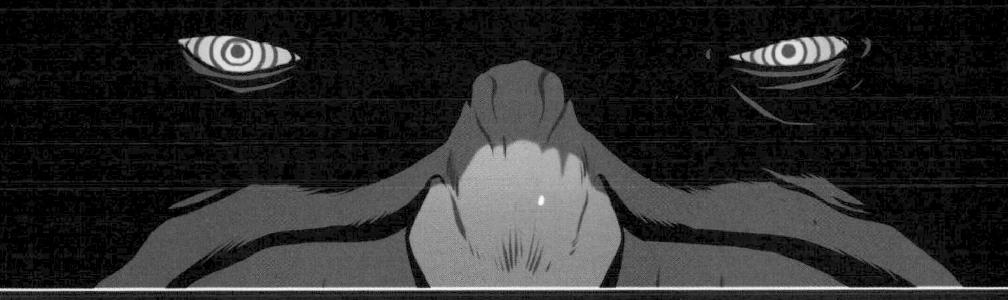
YOU BOYS SHOULDN'T BE OUTSIDE PLAYING HIDE-AND-SEEK IN THE MIDDLE OF THE NIGHT. IT'S FORTUNATE YOU'D GROWN WEARY AND WENT BACK TO BED BEFORE ONE OF YOU RAN INTO A TREE. OH NO, ONE OF YOU DID RUN INTO A TREE.

RETURN NOW, TO YOUR BEDS.
WHEN YOU RISE IN THE MORNING, YOU WON'T REMEMBER **ANYTHING** FROM TONIGHT.

ALSO...YOU'LL BE GRIPPED WITH A STRONG DESIRE TO CHANGE YOUR RIDICULOUS HAIRSTYLES TO UH...SOMETHING...WELL, SOMETHING A LITTLE LESS HILARIOUS TO ME.

K.

DID YOU JUST HYPNOTIZE THEM...OR SOMETHING?
AH...YES, MY DEAR. I'M AFRAID IT'S A NECESSARY EVIL I MUST PERFORM FROM TIME TO TIME IN ORDER TO KEEP EVERYONE SAFE.
HYPNOTISM'S REAL?

I DON'T GET IT.

DON'T GET WHAT, CHILD?

WHY **SHOW** US ALL THIS AMAZING STUFF IF...IF YOU'RE JUST GOING TO HYPNOTIZE US TO **FORGET?**

I HAVE **NO** INTENTIONS OF HYPNOTIZING YOU YOUNG LADIES. I HONESTLY COULDN'T EVEN IF I WANTED TO.
AMONG MY... PEOPLE, I'M EXTREMELY PROFICIENT IN WHAT YOU CALL HYPNOSIS.
BUT...I'VE NEVER BEEN ABLE TO HYPNOTIZE FEMALES.
BESIDES, I SUSPECT YOU THREE CAN BE TRUSTED.

YOU KNOW, THIS IS THE THIRD YEAR IN A ROW I'VE HAD TO... WELL, LET'S JUST SAY THE STUMP TWINS HAVE **FORGOTTEN** MORE ABOUT THIS ISLAND THAN I FEEL COMFORTABLE WITH ADMITTING TO.

PLEASE STAY CLEAR OF THAT OLD WELL. IT'S **NOT** SAFE.
WE WILL.

I CAN'T BELIEVE IT'S ALL **REAL**. HE'S SO... I MEAN, HE ALWAYS ACTS LIKE...
WHO?
PEOPLE. JUST PEOPLE, ACT LIKE HE'S A MONSTER OR SOMETHING.
SUPER TIRED.
ME TOO, BUT THAT WAS AWESOME!

SOMETHING **STILL** DOESN'T MAKE SENSE.

WHAT DOESN'T MAKE SENSE?
ELRIC SAID HE TOOK THE SNACKS, RIGHT?
BUT... WELL, WHATEVER I SAW THAT NIGHT WASN'T MR. ELRIC. IT WAS SHADOWY AND KINDA MISTY.
WHY WOULD HE MAKE THAT UP?
YOU WERE HALF ASLEEP. YOU SAID IT, YOURSELF.
BAD NEWS.
LOOKS LIKE WE'RE CRAWLING IN SPIDERWEBS, AGAIN.

BREAKFAST
ACCORDING TO THE JOURNAL ELRIC GAVE ME, ALL THOSE WEIRD MARKINGS EVERYWHERE ARE GNOMISH RUNES!
THEY'RE WHAT?
GNOME WRITING.
BUT I CAN'T FIND ANY KIND OF TRANSLATION IN HERE.
SO...BIGFOOT. DIDN'T SEEM SO BLOOD-THIRSTY TO ME.
KINDA THE OPPOSITE.
ELRIC SAID HE'S A VEGETARIAN.
HE'S MORE LIKE A BIG PUPPY OR SOMETHING, RIGHT?
HE'S SMART. ELRIC TAUGHT HIM SIGN LANGUAGE. DOGS CAN'T DO THAT.

I JUST MEAN HE SEEMS SO GENTLE IS ALL.
HE'S NOT THE BEAST SOME PEOPLE CLAIM HE IS.
AND HEY, IF BIGFOOT'S REAL, MAYBE VAMPIRES ARE, TOO?
WHO VANTS MORE BROWN FOODS FOR CHILDRENS?
VAMPIRES. CHECK.
TOTALLY.

BOOM

I KNOW YOU'VE BEEN SNEAKING OUT AT NIGHT.
I DON'T KNOW HOW YOU'RE DOING IT...YET, BUT I'M GONNA FIND OUT, AND WHEN I DO--

SOUNDS LIKE YOU MIGHT HAVE BEEN DREAMING, CALLIE.
I DID SEE YOU SLEEPWALKING.

NICE TRY, BUT I KNOW WHAT I SAW.
YOU WERE ALL GONE.
AGAIN!

NO WAY.
YOU WERE TALKING ABOUT DANCING WITH POSSUMS.
THEN YOU PICKED UP YOUR CHAIR AND CREATED A FIRE HAZARD IN THE DOORWAY.

WHAT IF THERE HAD BEEN A FIRE, CALLIE?
SO...WHAT'S UP WITH ALL THE POSSUM STUFF?

YOU LOOK TIRED, CALLIE.
YOU SHOULD TRY TO TAKE A NAP.

LATER THAT DAY
I HAD BEEN HUNTING THIS HAIRY CREATURE ALL NIGHT, AND I **FINALLY** HAD THE BEAST CORNERED...

WHERE WAS THIS, AGAIN?

WHA...OH, MONTANA.
NOW, **IF** I MAY CONTINUE?
THERE I WAS--

WHERE IN MONTANA?
MY AUNT LIVES THERE.
THE...UPPER ...PART?
SOMEWHERE IN THAT UPPER PART. NOW, WHERE WAS I?

OH, YOU MEAN THE CHINCHILLA FOREST!

YES, THAT'S THE ONE. IT WAS VERY--

I JUST MADE THAT UP.
THERE'S NO SUCH PLACE.
I MUST HAVE BEEN MISTAKEN.

MY DAD SAYS ONLY **FOOLS** BELIEVE IN BIGFOOT.
IS THAT TRUE?

SON, I **SERIOUSLY** DOUBT YOUR DAD HAS RESEARCHED THE TOPIC AS THOROUGHLY AS I HAVE. I CAN ASSURE YOU THAT BIGFOOT IS **DEFINITELY** REAL.

WHERE'S ALL YOUR PROOF?
GOOD QUESTION, BRO.
WELL, I HAVE PLASTER CASTS OF ITS FOOTPRINTS, FOR STARTERS.
NOW--
THOSE ARE PROBABLY AS **FAKE** AS YOUR STORIES!
MY OFFICE...
NOW!

WELP...THAT'S NOT GOOD.
I HOPE HE DOESN'T GET SENT HOME.
I'M MORE WORRIED ABOUT HIM TELLING TOOTER ABOUT LAST NIGHT.
HE WOULDN'T DO THAT.
ARE YOU SURE?
HEY, CHECK OUT EMMA?
EMMA!
WAKE UP!

SO...CARROTS, BREAD, MILK WITH NO STRAW AND... A BIG OLD SQUIRT OF KETCHUP?
THIS IS... DINNER?
WHAT DO YOU THINK HAPPENED TO THE COOK?
CALLIE SAID SHE WAS FIRED AND SENT HOME?
WHAT? THERE'S LIKE, TWO DAYS OF CAMP LEFT.
WHY FIRE HER, NOW?
WHY NOT JUST WAIT?
MAYBE SHE TURNED INTO A BAT AND, YOU KNOW, FLEW AWAY?
MAYBE RAND TOLD TOOTER SHE WAS A VAMPIRE?

C'MON.
I NEED TO TALK TO MR. ELRIC ABOUT THIS.

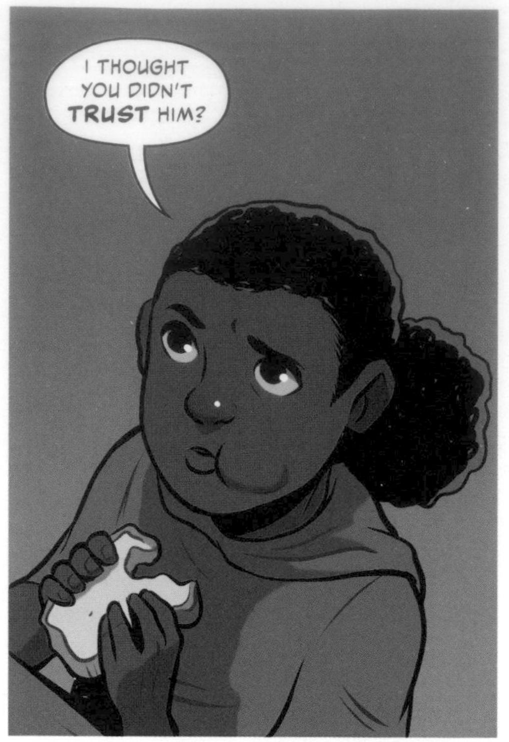

I THOUGHT YOU DIDN'T **TRUST** HIM?

I DON'T, BUT SOMETHING FEELS **OFF** ABOUT THIS WHOLE THING.

I THINK I'M GONNA HANG BACK HERE.

YOU KNOW, TO KEEP AN EYE OUT FOR RAND.

GOOD IDEA. WE'LL BE BACK AS SOON AS WE CAN.

KNOCK
KNOCK
I DON'T THINK HE'S HERE, WIL.
WHY EXACTLY ARE WE BOTHERING MR. ELRIC ABOUT THIS?
BECAUSE **IF** SHE REALLY **IS** A VAMPIRE AND TOOTER **DID** DO SOMETHING TO HER, HE'S GONNA WANT TO KNOW.

HE MUST BE IN THE FOREST. COME ON.

YOU GUYS SEE UP THERE, WHERE THE TREES COME TOGETHER AT THE TOPS?

THAT'S WHERE THE CHICKCHARNEES BUILD THEIR NESTS.
THOSE **BIRD** THINGS?

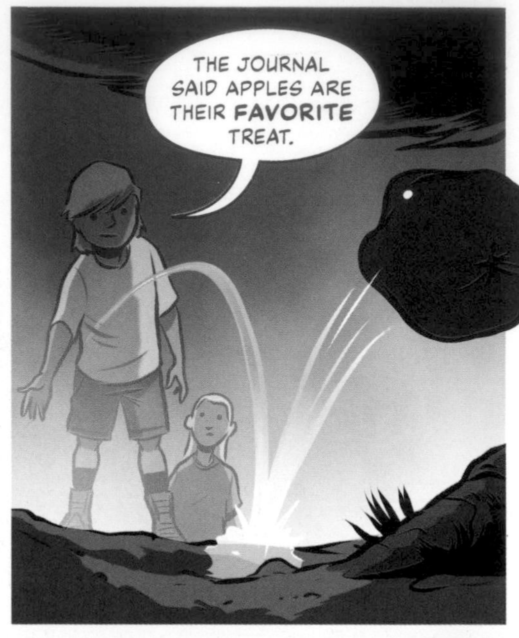
THE JOURNAL SAID APPLES ARE THEIR **FAVORITE** TREAT.

WHY ARE YOU GIVING **THEM** TREATS AFTER THEY **ATTACKED** US?
THEY WERE ONLY DEFENDING THEIR HOME, VIOLET.

FWOOSH

TCHK

HELLO, THERE.

I SEE YOU'VE BEEN READING THE JOURNAL.

WE WERE UH... LOOKING FOR YOU, AND WE THOUGHT YOU MIGHT BE OUT HERE.
WHAT ARE YOU DOING WITH THAT GARDEN GNOME?
FAILING.
THE COOK'S MISSING. WE THINK MR. TOOTER MAY HAVE **DISCOVERED** SHE WAS REALLY A VAMPIRE AND...AND HE MIGHT HAVE...**DONE** SOMETHING TO HER?
TIBBLES?
OH, **HEAVENS** NO.
THEY'RE... I MEAN, **SHE'S** A BIT **ODD**, BUT SHE'S...
WELL, SHE'S **NOT** A VAMPIRE, I ASSURE YOU.

I'M SURE THERE'S A PERFECTLY REASONABLE EXPLANATION FOR HER ABSENCE, GIRLS.

CALLIE, OUR COUNSELOR, SAID SHE WAS FIRED.
BUT NOBODY KNOWS WHY.

IF IT WILL EASE YOUR MINDS, I'LL LOOK INTO THE MATTER.

THERE'S SOMETHING I NEED TO ASK YOU.
ASK AWAY.

YOU SAID IT WAS **YOU** WHO TOOK THE SNACKS?
BUT I SAW SOMETHING IN OUR CABIN THAT NIGHT, AND IT **WASN'T** YOU.
IT WAS LIKE A SMOKY SHADOW OR SOMETHING.

YOU'RE CERTAINLY NOT THE FIRST PERSON TO TELL ME I HAVE A RATHER SPOOKY SHADOW.
YEAH, I CAN KINDA SEE THAT.
UH...
RUSTLE
SNAP
ELRIC!

MR. ELRIC, SIR! LADY MIM HAS SENT ME WITH URGENT NEWS.
THE HUMAN, CLARENCE TOOTER, HAS CALLED AN EMERGENCY CAMP MEETING EFFECTIVE IMMEDIATELY.
SHE FEARS THE WORST.
THANK YOU, TURNIP.
GIRLS, RETURN TO CAMP AT ONCE. TOOTER CANNOT DISCOVER YOU'RE MISSING.
LADY MIM'S INTUITION IS RARELY WRONG. I URGE CAUTION.
WHAT ARE YOU GOING TO DO?
A REAL GNOME!
WE SHALL SEE.

THAT WAS A REAL-LIFE GNOME!
WE KNOW, WE KNOW.
YOU DO?
SHH...WE'RE GETTING CLOSE TO CAMP.

I'LL NOT DISCUSS THIS FURTHER. PLEASE LEAVE!
IT'S COMING FROM THE FIRST-AID CABIN
SOUNDS LIKE ARGUING.

THAT WAS A REAL GNOME! IT WAS--
WE'LL DISCUSS IT LATER, EM. FOR NOW, HUSH.
I'M PRETTY SURE THAT'S TOOTER IN THERE.

YOU'VE GONE TOO FAR, CLARENCE! I'LL NOT LET YOU PLACE THE CAMPERS IN DANGER!
WELL, YOU'RE NOT THE ONE IN CHARGE, NURSE!
THEY SOUND REALLY ANGRY.
SHOULD WE DO SOMETHING?
LIKE WHAT, VI?
GO KNOCK ON THE DOOR AND MAKE THEM HUG IT OUT?
SOUNDS LIKE IT STOPPED, ANYWAY.

IT'S TOOTER.

WHAT'S HE HOLDING?

WHERE'S NURSE MIM? SHE WOULD **NEVER** LET HIM TAKE TOAST.

HE TOOK... HER TOAST?

DO YOU THINK HE KNOWS?

I DOUBT IT.

I'M **SO** CONFUSED.

WE'LL HAVE TO FIGURE IT OUT LATER.

RIGHT NOW, WE NEED TO GET **BACK** TO CAMP AND FIND OUT WHAT'S REALLY GOING ON.

MAYBE MOLLY KNOWS SOMETHING.

SHORTLY
ATTENTION, CAMPERS AND COUNSELORS.
I'VE RECEIVED SOME **ALARMING** INFORMATION FROM A VERY RELIABLE SOURCE.
IT APPEARS THERE'S A LARGE, DANGEROUS **BEAR** IN THE FOREST NEARBY.
Boi

AND, AS IF THAT WASN'T BAD ENOUGH, IT APPEARS THAT SOME OF THE CAMPERS HAVE, IN FACT, BEEN **FEEDING** IT.

AS A RESULT, I'VE SET A CURFEW, EFFECTIVE **IMMEDIATELY** FOR **ALL** CAMPERS **AND** COUNSELORS TO RETURN TO THEIR CABINS AND REMAIN THERE UNTIL FURTHER NOTICE.

ANYONE FOUND IN **VIOLATION** OF SAID CURFEW WILL BE SENT HOME **IMMEDIATELY.**

YOU HAVE EXACTLY THREE MINUTES TO BE IN YOUR CABINS, SO I CAN TAKE CARE OF THIS... BEAR, IN A CHILD-FREE ENVIRONMENT.
YOU!
WILLOW, I'M GLAD I FOUND YOU.
I NEED TO TELL YOU...

OOMPH
SLAM

WHAT DID YOU SAY, RAND?
WHAT DID YOU TELL HIM?
GRRGET OFF ME!
THAT'S ENOUGH, BOTH OF YOU!
EVERYONE TO YOUR DESIGNATED CABINS. NOW!
CHILL, WIL.
NOT COOL, BRO.
WHAT THE HECK?

HOLD ON!
I NEED TO TELL YOU SOMETHING.

MAYBE YOU SHOULD GO TELL YOUR NEW **BESTIE**. I'M SURE HE'LL BE **HAPPY** TO LISTEN.

MAYBE I WILL!

C'MON, BRO.

THANKS AGAIN, PETE. THERE'S **NO** WAY **I'M** FALLING ASLEEP TONIGHT.
WELL, JUST BE CAREFUL WITH THAT STUFF, CALLIE.
IT CAN CAUSE...TUMMY TROUBLE.
HOW **COULD** RAND EVEN KNOW ABOUT THATCH?
ELRIC HYPNOTIZED HIM, OR WHATEVER.
MAYBE IT DIDN'T WORK?
RAND **WAS** IN HIS OFFICE, AND NOW SUDDENLY TOOTER IS WARNING US ABOUT A BEAR?
I DON'T BUY IT.
BUT **STILL,** THAT DOESN'T EXPLAIN **WHY** RAND WOULD DO IT.
MAYBE HE DIDN'T MEAN TO?
MAYBE IT JUST SLIPPED OUT OR SOMETHING?
TOOTER CAN BE INTIMIDATING WHEN HE WANTS TO BE.
I MEAN, HE SEEMS KINDA THAT WAY TO ME, ANYWAY.

I DON'T WANT TO BELIEVE IT EITHER, YOU GUYS, BUT I CAN'T THINK OF A BETTER EXPLANATION.
SO...WHAT DO WE DO, NOW?

I CERTAINLY HOPE YOU GIRLS AREN'T PLANNING ON SNEAKING OUT AGAIN TONIGHT.

GLUG GLUG

CRAZY COFFEE

YOU KEEP DRINKING THOSE COFFEE DRINKS, AND YOU'RE NOT GONNA BE ABLE TO SLEEP AT ALL TONIGHT.
THAT'S THE IDEA. I ACTUALLY HATE COFFEE, BUT I'M NOT LETTING YOU GIRLS OUT OF MY SIGHT AGAIN.
DID YOU KNOW THAT COFFEE ACTS AS A NATURAL LAXATIVE? ESPECIALLY FOR PEOPLE WHO DON'T NORMALLY DRINK IT MUCH.
OH, NO, CALLIE, POO POO!
I'M SURE I'LL BE FINE, GIRLS. THANKS FOR YOUR CONCERN.

TWO HOURS LATER
AND...HERE COMES THE POO-CHOO TRAIN.
GURGLE BLURG
LOST IN POSSUM TOWN

OH, JEEZY...
OH, NO...
GURGLE

I **HATE** USING THE RESTROOMS AFTER DARK.
I JUST **KNOW** THERE'S GONNA BE A BIG OL' SPIDER IN THERE!

OKAY, SHE'S GONE.
LET'S GO!

MAYBE THIS IS A **BAD** IDEA, YOU GUYS.
TOOTER SEEMED PRETTY SERIOUS ABOUT THE CURFEW.

STAY IF YOU WANT, MOLLY.
MAYBE CALLIE'LL TELL YOU SOME POSSUM STORIES.
WE NEED TO FIND MR. ELRIC.
WE SHOULD PROBABLY SPLIT UP,

ARE YOU **CRAZY?**
WHAT ABOUT FOG LEECHES?
YEAH, WHAT ABOUT FOG LEECHES?

OKAY, FIRST OFF, THERE'S NO SUCH THING AS FOG LEECHES, MOLLY!
SECONDLY, I'VE GIVEN IT A LOT OF THOUGHT, AND I THINK IF TOOTER HASN'T GONE AFTER THATCH YET, MAYBE WE CAN DELAY HIM A LITTLE.
I THINK THE BEST PLAN IS FOR ME AND MOLLY TO FIND TOOTER WHILE EMMA AND VIOLET LOOK FOR MR. ELRIC.
SOUNDS DANGEROUS.

MAYBE MOLLY'S RIGHT. MAYBE WE SHOULDN'T GET INVOLVED.
WE COULD JUST LET THE OTHER ADULTS HANDLE IT.

OTHER ADULTS? WHAT OTHER ADULTS, VIOLET?
NOBODY'S SEEN NURSE MIM SINCE TOOTER LEFT HER CABIN-- WITH TOAST, BY THE WAY-- WHICH IS SOMETHING SHE'D NEVER ALLOW IF SHE COULD STOP IT.
AND OH YEAH, THE COOK'S GONE, TOO!

WELL, NOW THAT YOU PUT IT THAT WAY, I'M EVEN MORE TERRIFIED!
SHE'S RIGHT, YOU GUYS.

I'M SCARED, TOO, BUT WE CAN'T SIT BACK WHILE TOOTER HURTS THATCH...OR ANYONE ELSE.
I'LL GO GET ELRIC, WILLOW.

I'LL COME WITH YOU!
OKAY.

WHAT ABOUT YOU, MOLLY?
I COULD USE SOME BACKUP.

YEAH, OKAY, BUT I...
I MEAN...SO I JUST WANTED TO SAY THAT, YOU KNOW...IN CASE WE GET BUSTED...
THERE'S THIS **THING** I KINDA NEED TO TELL YOU AND--

WOW, MOLLY. THAT'S A **BUNCH** OF DRAMA.
YOU SURE YOU'RE FEELING **OKAY?**

SORRY. I GET WEIRD WHEN I'M TIRED.
IT CAN WAIT UNTIL LATER.

LATER
THERE HE IS.
WHAT'S HE DOING?
IT'S BAIT. HE MUST BE TRYING TO **LURE** THATCH INTO THE CAMP.
SO, WHAT NOW?
PLAN B.
WHAT'S PLAN B?

WAIT...PLAN B IS BREAKING INTO TOOTER'S CABIN? ARE YOU CRAZY?

IT'S NOT BREAKING IN IF IT'S TOTALLY UNLOCKED.
JUST STAY OUT HERE AND BE MY LOOKOUT.
THIS IS A BAD, BAD, BAD, AWFUL IDEA, WILLOW.
WE HAVE TO TRY SOMETHING. MAYBE THERE'S A PHONE IN THERE I CAN USE TO CALL FOR HELP.

THERE'S NO PHONE, TRUST ME.
HOW DO YOU KNOW?
A HUNCH?

EITHER WAY, I KNOW HE HAS TOAST IN THERE.

IF YOU'RE THAT HUNGRY, LET'S JUST SNEAK INTO THE LUNCH CABIN, INSTEAD.
NOT THAT KIND OF TOAST. I'LL EXPLAIN LATER.

SMELLS LIKE OLD CHEESE IN HERE.
AND IT LOOKS LIKE MOLLY WAS RIGHT ABOUT THE PHONE.
WELL, WHERE IS HE AT?
IF I WERE A GNOME, WHERE WOULD I--
THERE YOU ARE!
LET'S JUST GET YOU BACK TO...
WHAT THE...?
WHAT IS... WEREWOLVES?
WHY WOULD HE BE RESEARCHING WEREWOLVES?
WERWULF

WEREWOLVES?
TOOTER'S **WAY** OFF ON THIS ONE.

click

I REALLY DON'T CARE, YOUNG LADY!
WE'LL DISCUSS IT IN THE MORNING. NOW, GET BACK TO YOUR CABIN THIS INSTANT!

I'M TIRED OF EVERYONE TELLING ME WHAT TO DO AROUND HERE.
STUPID NURSE! STUPID DAUGHTER!
STUPID EVERYONE!

IT'S GONNA BE A **BUSY** NIGHT.
I'M FINALLY GOING TO GET THE ULTIMATE PRIZE--AND ANYTHING ELSE I COME ACROSS OUT THERE.
THIS ISLAND'S CRAWLING WITH TROPHIES!
SHOOK
SHOWTIME.
TOAST!
WAKE UP!

WHERE...OH, HELLO, MISS WILLOW.
WE'RE IN A REAL PICKLE HERE, PAL
YES, I'VE LONG SUSPECTED THIS IS WHAT THE INSIDE OF A PICKLE LOOKS LIKE.
WHAT? I MEAN, TOAST, I NEED YOU TO GO CHECK ON NURSE MIM. I'M WORRIED SHE MIGHT BE IN DANGER. NOBODY'S SEEN HER SINCE SHE CONFRONTED TOOTER EARLIER.
OH, DEAR.
AND I NEED TO FIND...WELL, SOME KIND OF A DISTRACTION, AND FAST.
WHAT KIND OF DISTRACTION?
I'M... NOT REALLY SURE.
IT NEEDS TO BE BIG OR...LOUD. OR BOTH!
HAVE YOU CONSIDERED A DRAGON?
DO YOU HAVE A DRAGON I COULD BORROW, TOAST?
NO, BUT MY COUSIN BINGO MIGHT.
SHHF

PREPOSTEROUS!
WHERE?
BINGO!
I MEANT, I FOUND SOMETHING.
ALAS. I THOUGHT THE VERY MENTION OF HIS NAME SPIRITED HIM TO US, HERE, INSIDE THIS DREADFUL PICKLE!
SO...YOU THINK FINDING YOUR COUSIN IN A DESK DRAWER IS MORE PREPOSTEROUS THAN WHAT YOU JUST SAID?
AND AGAIN, WE'RE NOT INSIDE A... NEVERMIND.
C'MON, YOU SILLY GNOME. WE NEED TO HURRY...
WHAT?
THUCK

WHY'S MOLLY IN A PHOTO WITH TOOTER...
47TH ANNUAL FATHER DAUGHTER GRAND HUNT
...AT A FATHER-DAUGHTER HUNT?

47TH ANNUAL FATHER DAUGHTER GRAND HUNT

RAND...

MOLLY!

WHAT'S A MOLLY?
IT'S SOMETHING THAT **LIES** TO YOU AND THEN **STABS** YOU IN THE BACK.
OH, I DON'T THINK I LIKE THE SOUND OF THAT.

DO YOU SEE TOOTER ANYWHERE, PAL?

I'M TOO SHORT TO SEE OVER THE FOG.

IT'S OKAY, I SEE HIM OVER THERE.
MAYBE YOU SHOULD GO CHECK ON NURSE MIM, TOAST.
I'LL STAY A BIT LONGER, IN CASE YOU NEED ASSISTANCE.

SEEMS LIKE A PRETTY **SILLY** TRAP FROM SUCH A SELF-PROCLAIMED **LEGENDARY** HUNTER, IF YOU ASK ME.

OR PERHAPS BRILLIANT, I FEAR.
THATCH IS KNOWN TO LET HIS STOMACH GET HIM INTO ALL SORTS OF BAD SITUATIONS.

LET'S GET CLOSER.
CLOSER?
LADY WILLOW! THATCH IS HERE!
I SAW. HURRY!
THAT'S IT, MY BIG, HAIRY FRIEND. JUST A FEW MORE STEPS.

HERE WE GO.
FWISHHH
CRIK
SSSSSSSSSSSSS

AHH!
BOOOOM
CRACK
CRACK
CRACK
CRACK
CRACK
IEEE!
CRACK
CRACK
CRACK
CRACK
CRACK
AM I DEAD? IS THIS DEATH?
DID I POOP 'EM?
YES.

YOU!

RUN, TOAST!

CONFOUND YOU, GIRL!
THIS IS NO TIME FOR PRANKS!

YOU GET BACK HERE, RIGHT NOW!

THIS GNOME WAS IN MY OFFICE, THIEF! GET BACK HERE!
I DON'T WANT TO!
LEAVE ME ALONE!
DID THAT GROUNDSKEEPER PUT YOU UP TO THIS BECAUSE HE'S TOO SCARED TO--
UMMPH
FOOOMMP
RIPPP

I KNOW YOU'RE PROTECTING THIS ISLAND OF FREAKS--
SMASH
WILLOW! WE FOUND ELRIC!
I SEE THAT.

HSSS
WHAT... WHAT ARE YOU?
JUST ANOTHER FREAK.
NO! PLEASE, NO!
HSSSSSSS
STOP!
DON'T HURT MY DAD, YOU MONSTER!

PLEASE...
PLEASE...
WHAT'VE I DONE?

I LOST MYSELF...

FORGIVE ME.

WOOOSH

THE SHOW'S **OVER.** GET TO YOUR CABIN, MOLLY. WE'LL HAVE **WORDS** IN THE MORNING.
YES, SIR.
AND AS FOR YOU THREE...
MY OFFICE, **NOW!**
I THINK IT'S TIME WE HAVE A LITTLE DISCUSSION ABOUT MINDING YOUR OWN BUSINESS.
PROTECTING THIS ISLAND FROM YOU **IS** OUR BUSINESS, TOOTER.
YOU'LL HAVE TO LOCK US UP TO STOP US.

KACHUNG
YOU WON'T GET AWAY WITH THIS, WE'RE JUST KIDS!

I'M ALREADY GETTING AWAY WITH IT, GIRL.
IN FACT, I'VE BEEN GETTING AWAY WITH IT ALL WEEK.

WHY DO YOU EVEN HAVE A SECRET ROOM WITH A GIANT STEEL CAGE ANYWAY?

YOU'D NEED TO ASK THE FORMER CAMP LEADER. TOO BAD SHE'S... EXPIRED.
MAYBE YOUR FRIEND KURT HAS SOME IDEAS?
NOW, IF YOU'LL EXCUSE ME. I HAVE A HUNT TO PREPARE FOR.
YOU CAN'T JUST LEAVE US IN HERE, TOOTER!

SLAM

THIS IS **SO BAD**, YOU GUYS.
I'M WORRIED ABOUT THATCH.
YOU SHOULD BE, FLOWER GIRL.

WHO... WHO SAID THAT.

I DID, PURPLE PRINCESS.

KURT?
WHAT ARE **YOU** DOING IN HERE? TOOTER SAID HE SENT YOU HOME.

WH...WHY'S YOUR HAIR SO LONG?
I'M CHAINED TO A WALL IN A CAGE FOR FOUR DAYS, AND YOU'RE WORRIED ABOUT MY HAIR STYLE?
BUT WHY DID HE PUT YOU IN HERE? DID HE DO THAT TO YOUR CLOTHES, TOO?
UH, NO. THE CLOTHES I DID MYSELF.
AND IF I'M BEING HONEST, IT'S ALSO WHY I'M LOCKED IN HERE.
BUT THE STUMP TWINS HAVE DONE FAR WORSE THAN YOU DID AND HE DIDN'T LOCK THEM UP LIKE THIS.
YEAH, WELL, THEY PROBABLY DIDN'T GET ANGRY AND GO A LITTLE WOLFY, EITHER.
MY AUNT IS GONNA EAT ME ALIVE.
WOLFY?
SO...PEOPLE IN MY FAMILY HAVE SOME KINDA UNIQUE...ISSUES, AND TOOTER PROVOKED ME. HE DIDN'T LIKE WHAT HE SAW... AND HERE I AM.

KURT, WE HAVE TO GET OUT OF HERE AND FIND ELRIC RIGHT NOW.
LET ME KNOW HOW THAT GOES. I'LL BE OVER HERE TAKING ANOTHER NAP.
YOU'D RATHER TAKE A **NAP** THAN FIND A WAY OUT OF HERE?
DO YOU REALLY THINK WE DIDN'T TRY **EVERYTHING?**
THIS CAGE WAS BUILT TO HOLD STRONGER THINGS THAN **US**, SO UNLESS YOU'VE GOT THE KEY, I SUGGEST YOU PULL UP SOME HAY AND GET COMFY.
KCHINK
DID YOU SAY "WE"?
OVER THERE.
IT'S...THE COOK.
THEY TOLD US SHE GOT FIRED.

HELLO TO CHILDRENS.
I'M SO SORRY, MA'AM.
IT'S POSSIBLE TOOTER LOCKED YOU UP BECAUSE... BECAUSE WE WERE MAKING JOKES ABOUT YOU BEING...A VAMPIRE.
TOOTER'S A REAL FOOL IF HE BELIEVES THAT.
THEY'RE CLEARLY GOBLINS STACKED UP UNDER A DRESS.
I NEVER BELIEVED IT, EITHER--
WAIT, WHAT?
GOBLINS?
I SWEAR, YOU HUMANS WALK AROUND EVERY DAY IN A TOWN FILLED WITH MAGIC AND WONDER, YET SOMEHOW YOU'RE TOTALLY OBLIVIOUS TO ALL OF IT.
IT'S KIND OF HILARIOUS.
YOU'RE LUCKY I DON'T BITE.

BECAUSE... YOU'RE A WEREWOLF?
FULL-BLOODED.
AND YOUR BROTHER, RAND?
NOW YOU'RE CATCHING ON.
BUT...IT WASN'T A FULL MOON.
HEY, DON'T BELIEVE EVERYTHING YOU SEE IN MOVIES, BLONDIE.
A FULLY MATURE WEREWOLF CAN CHANGE WHENEVER THEY WANT, ESPECIALLY WHEN THEY'RE MAD.
I GUESS YOU CAN SEE WHAT THAT GOT ME.
CHILDRENS NEED TO HAVE THE SLEEPING REST.
THEY'RE RIGHT.
BESIDES, YOU'RE NOT GOING ANYWHERE. MIGHT AS WELL GET SOME SLEEP IF YOU CAN.

THE NEXT MORNING
thump
thump

thump

bang

WAKE UP. TOOTER'S BACK.

WILLOW?
ARE YOU GUYS IN THERE?
BOOM
BOOM
BOOM
EMMA?
VIOLET?
IS ANYBODY BACK THERE? IT'S RAND!

RAND!
WE'RE HERE!
TOOTER LOCKED US IN A CAGE AND KURT'S WITH US!
AND THE COOK!

THE DOOR'S LOCKED, AND I FOUND A KEY, BUT IT'S NOT THE ONE FOR THIS DOOR.
EVERYBODY STAND BACK, I HAVE AN IDEA.
JUST...TRY NOT TO FREAK OUT, OKAY?
TOO LATE!
JUST DO IT!
SMASH
TOOTER TOLD THE COUNSELORS HE CAUGHT YOU BREAKING CURFEW AND SENT YOU GUYS HOME!
I KNEW HE WAS LYING.
THIS KEY HAS TO BE FOR THAT CAGE, RIGHT?
HI, KURT.
I'LL GET YOU ALL OUT, BUT WE HAVE A HUGE PROBLEM.

DANG, DUDE, YOU **REALLY** DESTROYED THIS PLACE.
I DIDN'T DO THIS. I THINK IT WAS **TOOTER.**
WHY WOULD TOOTER DO THIS TO HIS **OWN** CABIN?
TOOTER MANS WAS CRAFTING WEAPONS, ME'S THINKING.
THATCH IS IN **SERIOUS** TROUBLE, GUYS.
I DON'T THINK HE WENT AFTER THATCH, WIL.
HOW DO YOU KNOW ABOUT THATCH?!
ELRIC SAID HE **HYPNOTIZED** YOU GUYS.

OH, HE TRIED. JUST LIKE EVERY SUMMER. TROUBLE IS, IT ONLY WORKS ON MORTALS...AND I'M A--
WEREWOLF?
YEAH, YOUR BROTHER ALREADY TOLD US ABOUT YOUR...FAMILY.

IF HE DIDN'T GO AFTER THATCH, WHERE IS HE?

TOOTER MAN'S HUNTING FRIEND ELRIC.

HE LEFT BEFORE DAWN WITH MOLLY. THEY HAD LOTS OF POINTY, WOODEN WEAPONS. THE KIND YOU HUNT VAMPIRES WITH. AND THERE'S MORE BAD NEWS!

HOLD THAT THOUGHT, RAND.
TOAST, WAKE UP!!

SO...YOU KNOW ABOUT GNOMES?
I'VE MET A VAMPIRE, WEREWOLF BROTHERS, AND A STACK OF GOBLINS, RAND. IS IT REALLY **SO** SURPRISING I KNOW ABOUT GNOMES, AS WELL?
M'LADY WILLOW, IT APPEARS WE'RE BACK INSIDE THE PICKLE AGAIN?
WHERE IS MIM?
THAT'S THE **OTHER** BAD NEWS.
WE FOUND NURSE MIM ON THE FLOOR IN HER CABIN, SURROUNDED BY SOME WEIRD-LOOKING MUSHROOMS. WE CAN'T GET HER TO WAKE UP.
THOSE ARE ETERNAL SLUMBER MUSHROOMS, I FEAR.
CLARENCE TOOTER IS CUNNING TO HAVE **LEARNED** OF THEIR POWER.
YOU CHILDREN MUST TAKE **EXTRA** CARE IF YOUR PLAN IS TO PURSUE HIM.

THE GOBLINS AND I WILL SEE TO MIM.
I'LL LET THE COUNSELORS KNOW WHAT'S GOING ON... TO A **DEGREE**.

RAND AND I'LL HEAD TO ELRIC'S CABIN.
WE'RE COMING, TOO.

LET'S BE FAST AND TRY **NOT** TO FREAK OUT ANY OTHER CAMPERS, OKAY.
THE GOBLINS SHOULD PROBABLY GET DRESSED.
GOOD IDEA FROM THE CHILDREN.
SO WEIRD.

SORRY I JUMPED TO CONCLUSIONS LAST NIGHT.
IT'S COOL. MAYBE NEXT TIME LET A GUY FINISH HIS SENTENCE BEFORE YOU KNOCK HIM DOWN?
DEAL.

WAIT.
TOOTER'S BEEN HERE. I CAN SMELL HIS STENCH.
EMMA, IS YOUR ARM BLEEDING?
JUST A LITTLE.
I JUST NEED A NEW BANDAGE

MR. ELRIC?

HE ISN'T HERE, WIL. NOW WHAT?
I GUESS WE KEEP LOOKING.

WELL, WHEREVER HE IS, IT'S A SAFE BET THAT TOOTER'S TRACKING HIM.
I NEED TO GET A FEW THINGS FROM MY CABIN BEFORE WE HEAD OUT.
HEAD OUT? ARE YOU **SERIOUS?** THEY'RE ARMED TO THE TEETH!
WE CAN WORRY ABOUT THAT WHEN WE FIND THEM.
MAYBE WE SHOULD WORRY ABOUT IT **NOW**.

SOON
HERE WE ARE... AGAIN, IN THE SCARY FOREST.
WATCH OUT FOR THE FOG LEECHES.

SO...THE STUFF YOU NEEDED TO GET FROM YOUR CABIN WAS A BOOK AND SOME FRUIT.
WHAT? WERE YOU EXPECTING A BATTLE-AXE?

YOU'RE A WEREWOLF, RAND. WHAT ARE YOU SO WORRIED ABOUT?
PLENTY OF STUFF. THOSE FOG LEECHES ARE NOTHING TO JOKE ABOUT, EITHER.

THEY'RE REAL?
UH...

THEY'RE VERY REAL, BUT DON'T WORRY.
THEY'RE NOT ATTRACTED TO HUMANS.

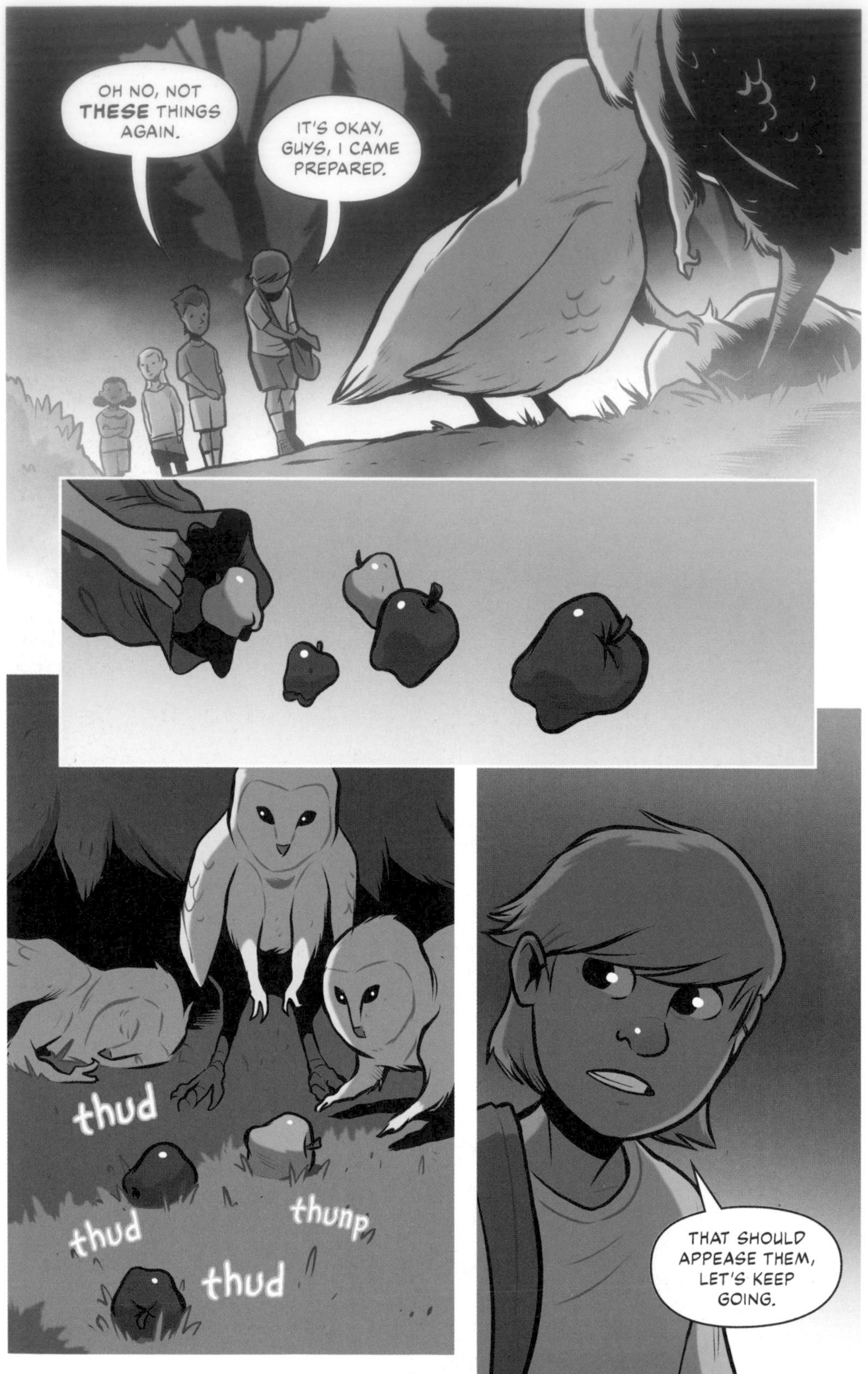
OH NO, NOT THESE THINGS AGAIN.
IT'S OKAY, GUYS, I CAME PREPARED.
thud
thud
thunp
thud
THAT SHOULD APPEASE THEM, LET'S KEEP GOING.

FRASH
GAH!
AHH!
SHEESH. HI, THATCH.
YOU SCARED THE **CHEESE** OUT OF ME, PAL.
ASK IF HE'S SEEN ELRIC.
GOOD IDEA, BRO.

THATCH, HAVE YOU SEEN MR. ELRIC? WE THINK HE'S IN SERIOUS DANGER.
WE **NEED** TO FIND HIM.
HE HASN'T SEEN HIM, EITHER.
mans walking not long gone.
AND...NOW THE BIRDS ARE TALKING.
bad mans hurt family.
small mans help.

LOOK, IT'S BEEN SHOT WITH AN ARROW.
THIS WAS TOOTER. IT HAD TO BE.
SNAP
RUSTLE

ELRIC'S IN FAR WORSE DANGER THAN WE THOUGHT.
WE NEED TO--
SNAP
YOU'RE CORRECT TO THINK THAT!
WHAA!!

FORGIVE ME, M'LADY.
C'MON, TOAST!
EVERYONE NEEDS TO **STOP** LEAPING OUT OF TREES AT ME, OR I'M GONNA START TYING **BELLS** TO **ALL** OF YOU.

IT WASN'T MY INTENTION TO FRIGHTEN, I ASSURE YOU.
I'D MERELY COME TO REPORT NURSE MIM IS RESPONDING WELL AND SHOULD MAKE A **FULL** RECOVERY.
BUT NOW I FEAR, HEARING YOUR CONVERSATION, THAT THE SITUATION WITH ELRIC IS GRAVER THAN I'D WANTED TO BELIEVE.
AND IF HE FEELS HE IS IN PERIL, NO DOUBT HE'LL FLEE TO THE CAVE OF DREAMING.
THAT SOUNDS... FAMILIAR.
sniff sniff
SHOO, THATCH. IT'S JUST ELRIC'S JOURNAL.
SO, WHERE'S THIS CAVE AT, TOAST?
NO IDEA! THIS ISLAND HOLDS **MANY** SECRETS.
FOUND IT!
THE CAVE OF DREAMING! AND THERE'S A **MAP!**
WHAT'S THE PART IN RED SAY?

THE RED... UH-OH...IT SAYS THE CAVE IS **FILLED** WITH THE ETERNAL SLUMBER MUSHROOMS...
Cave of Dreaming

"THEIR POLLEN MAKES LIVING CREATURES VERY SLEEPY AND SHOULD THEY FALL ASLEEP **INSIDE** THE CAVE, IT IS UNLIKELY..."

UNLIKELY WHAT?
IT'S UNLIKELY THEY WILL EVER WAKE UP AGAIN.

WHY WOULD HE GO TO A PLACE **SO** DANGEROUS, ESPECIALLY WHEN HE KNOWS THE RISKS?
BECAUSE, ELRIC'S A **VAMPIRE**. HE ISN'T A **LIVING** CREATURE, RIGHT?
I'D BET THAT CAVE WON'T AFFECT HIM AT ALL.
PRETTY CLEVER.

UH...GUYS. I'M LOOKING AT THIS MAP OF THE ISLAND AND...
...THIS CAVE IS A **LONG** WAY AWAY. ELRIC AND TOOTER HAVE A HUGE HEAD START ON US.
I DON'T THINK WE'LL BE ABLE TO REACH IT IN TIME TO DO ANYTHING.
WE HAVE TO TRY THOUGH, RIGHT?

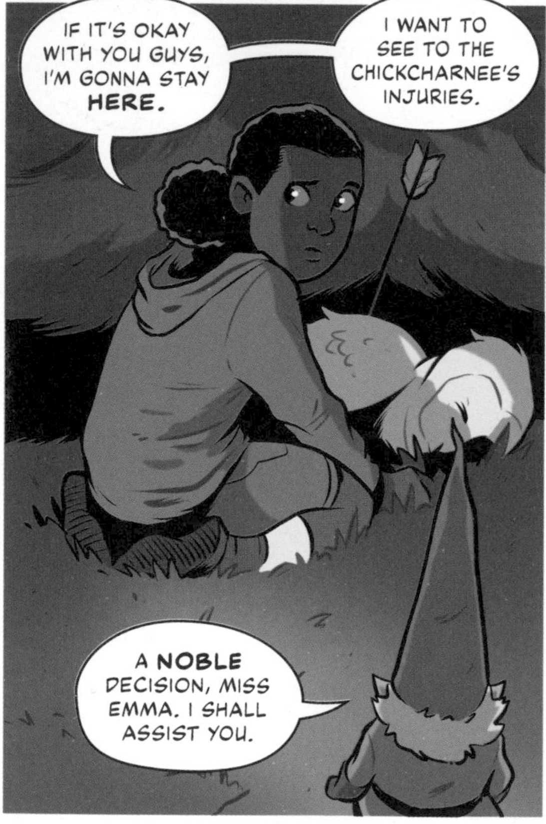
IF IT'S OKAY WITH YOU GUYS, I'M GONNA STAY **HERE.**
I WANT TO SEE TO THE CHICKCHARNEE'S INJURIES.
A **NOBLE** DECISION, MISS EMMA. I SHALL ASSIST YOU.

DO **NOT** TARRY, BRAVE CHILDREN, FOR YOUR OWN SAFETY. THERE ARE **FAR** WORSE THINGS TO ENCOUNTER IN THIS FOREST THAN CLARENCE TOOTER AFTER NIGHT FALLS.

WE CAN GO NORTH ON THIS BLUE LINE.
THAT'S A RIVER.

SCOOP

THATCH, WHAT ARE YOU DOING?
WE DON'T HAVE **TIME** FOR...

THIS!!

CRASH

HE'S **SO** FAST!

LEAP

SQUASH
SQUASH
SQUASH
I THINK WE'RE GETTING CLOSE. I SAW THESE HOLES ON THE MAP.!
DO YOU GUY SEE THOSE LIGHTS?
THEY'RE JUST WHISPS. AS LONG AS YOU DON'T FOLLOW THEM, THEY'RE HARMLESS.

SO... THIS IS THE CAVE, UH... PLACE?
ACCORDING TO THE MAP.

HEY, WHAT'S WRONG?
BAD PLACE.

YOU CAN STAY **HERE** IF YOU'RE SCARED.

I KNOW YOU'RE IN THERE, **VAMPIRE**.

THIS SEEMS LIKE A BAD IDEA, WIL.
YEP.

I **KNOW** YOU'RE HIDING FROM ME IN YOUR CAVE, BLOOD-SUCKER!
I AM **TRULY** ASHAMED OF MY BEHAVIOR LAST NIGHT, CLARENCE. YOU ATTACKED MY FRIENDS AND IN THAT MOMENT, I...LOST CONTROL.
FORTUNATELY FOR **ALL** OF US, I WAS ABLE TO REGAIN MY COMPOSURE.
BUT...IF YOU **CONTINUE** TO PURSUE ME, YOU **WILL** FACE ME AS MY **TRUE** SELF, AND I ASSURE YOU, IT WILL **NOT** END WELL FOR YOU.
YOU **DON'T** SCARE ME, DEVIL. I'VE DEALT WITH **WORSE** THAN YOU IN MY TRAVELS. AFTER I'VE TURNED YOU TO DUST, I'M GOING TO SCOUR THIS ISLAND UNTIL I'VE **DISCOVERED** EACH AND EVERY SECRET IT HOLDS.
CLICK
DON'T MOVE.
OH, LOOK GUYS, IT'S MOLLY THE TRAITOR.

BE QUIET AND LISTEN TO ME.
WHY SHOULD WE?
I DIDN'T TELL YOU HE WAS MY DAD BECAUSE I THOUGHT...YOU MIGHT STOP BEING MY FRIENDS.
GUESS WE'LL NEVER KNOW, NOW.
HE'S MY DAD AND I LOVE HIM, BUT HE'S GONE TOO FAR THIS TIME.
I TRIED TO STOP HIM, BUT HE'S OUT OF HIS MIND.
GRRR
SAYS THE GIRL POINTING A CROSSBOW AT US.
EASY, RAND. DON'T GET ALL WOLFY.
OH, THAT. IT ISN'T EVEN LOADED.
BUT, NOW THAT YOU'RE HERE, I THINK WE MIGHT BE ABLE TO AT LEAST GIVE ELRIC A CHANCE.
DO YOU EVEN HAVE A PLAN?
KINDA? DO YOU GUYS SEE THAT BAG ON THE GROUND?

HE HAS ALL OF HIS SUPPLIES IN THERE. IT'S HIS ANTI-VAMPIRE KIT. IT HAS HOLY WATER, WOODEN STAKES, FOOD AND EXTRA SUPPLIES.
AND HE TRAVELS AROUND WITH THIS STUFF JUST IN CASE HE HAS A RUN IN WITH A VAMPIRE?
PRETTY MUCH.

WHY SHOULD WE TRUST ANYTHING YOU SAY?

MY ENTIRE LIFE I'VE BEEN TOLD MONSTERS ARE VICIOUS CREATURES. THINGS TO BE FEARED. BUT... ELRIC'S A VAMPIRE...AND ONE OF THE KINDEST PEOPLE I'VE EVER MET.

AND THATCH...I'M JUST STARTING TO SERIOUSLY QUESTION EVERYTHING MY DAD'S TAUGHT ME.

BUT MORE IMPORTANTLY, I DON'T WANT THEM TO COME TO ANY HARM, NOT IF I CAN STOP IT.

WE NEED TO GET CLOSE ENOUGH SO WE CAN GET THE BAG AND THAT CROSSBOW AWAY FROM HIM.
UH, NO...I WAS JUST TALKING ABOUT THE BAG, THE CROSSBOW MIGHT BE TOO--
NAH, WE'LL GET THAT, TOO.
TRUST ME.

DAD!
LOOK WHO I FOUND **HIDING** BEHIND THESE ROCKS.
GOOD JOB, MOLLY.
WILLOW, COME OVER HERE, GIRL!
OH RIGHT, SORRY.
I SAID...
COME OVER HERE!
GET OVER HERE!
LET GO OF ME!

SURRENDER, VAMPIRE. SURRENDER TO ME OR THIS INNOCENT LITTLE GIRL WILL TAKE **YOUR** PLACE.

NOW WE SEE WHO THE **REAL** MONSTER IS.

VERY WELL, I SURRENDER UNDER THE CONDITION THAT THE GIRL **AND** HER FRIENDS DO NOT COME TO **ANY** HARM.

TSH FSH

DON'T YOU DO IT, MR.ELRIC! HE'S BLUFFING.

OH, I PROMISE YOU, VAMPIRE. I AM NOT BLUFFING.
TSH

YOU'LL NEED TO COME IN HERE, IF YOU INTEND TO FINISH ME YOURSELF.
ONE STEP INTO THE SUNLIGHT WILL TURN ME TO ASH, AND THEN WHERE WILL YOUR VICTORY BE?

HA
HA
HA
NICE TRY, BUT I THINK NOT. I SEE WHAT AWAITS ME INSIDE THAT CAVE OF YOURS.
I KNOW WHAT THOSE MUSHROOMS ARE CAPABLE OF.
SHHUMP
I USED THEM ON NURSE MIM LAST NIGHT.
THEY ARE CERTAINLY A DETERRENT.
BUT NO WORRIES, I'VE BROUGHT SOMETHING SPECIAL FOR THIS VERY SITUATION.
FLIP
HMM.
THAT'S... ODD. WHAT'S... WAIT...
shlup
WHERE'S ALL MY...
WHY IS IT SO MOIST IN HERE?

WHAT'S THIS, NOW?
WHAT IN THE...?
IS THIS FRENCH BREAD?

FEELS LIKE WARM MEATLOAF.
DID I PACK MEATLOAF?

IT'S LIKE A SOFT, **CHUNKY** TACO SALAD...
OR...A **REALLY** WET POTATO SALAD?
SMELLS LIKE IT'S SPOILED.

GROSS! IT'S **POOPIES!**

WAHHH!
SOMEONE POOPIED IN MY POUCH!
HEY!
GRAB
LET GO OF THAT, GIRL!
KACHUNK
OH!!

WILLOW!
NO!

UMPH... I'M OKAY. I THINK...
AHH!

EVERYONE STAY BACK!
JUST STAY BACK! THIS AIN'T OVER.
UMPH.

COWARD! HSSSS

YOU SEND CHILDREN TO FIGHT YOUR FIGHTS WHILE YOU HIDE IN YOUR FUNGUS CAVE SPIRITING POOP INTO MY FAVORITE POUCH, AND YOU CALL ME A COWARD?
NO!
NO!
YOU'RE ABOUT TO--

tonk

HOW DARE--
thunch

thud
HEY!

ROCK
DERP!

IT'S... TOAST!
ARE WE REALLY BEING RESCUED BY GNOMES RIDING OWL THINGIES?
TOTALLY.
OUCH.
DIRECT HIT, COBBLER!
GNOMES, STAY IN FORMATION AND FOLLOW ME!

SWOOSH
HEY!
PUT ME DOWN!
WAH!
NOT THE CAVE!
NOT THE CAVE!

OOMPH.

WELL, HELLO, CLARENCE.
I'M SO **VERY** PLEASED YOU'VE RECONSIDERED JOINING ME IN MY LITTLE CAVE.

I'M SO SEEPY...

I GOSSA POO HANDS ON MY HANDS.

YES, I SAW THAT. HOW VERY UNFORTUNATE.

NO! PLEASE.
PLEASE, MR. ELRIC.
BE AT EASE, MY DEAR.
I HAVE NO INTENTION OF HARMING YOUR MISERABLE FATHER.
I ONLY WISH TO HAVE A LITTLE CHAT WITH HIM AND TO TEACH HIM A FEW MANNERS.
I PROMISE TO HAVE HIM HOME BY SUNDOWN.
MOLLY! WE NEED YOUR HELP OVER HERE.
C'MON, VIOLET. I'M FINE.
WILLOW, YOU HAVE AN ARROW STICKING OUT OF YOUR BODY. YOU'RE NOT FINE.
INDEED, GIRL. WE NEED TO GET YOU TO NURSE MIM RIGHT AWAY, BUT FIRST, THE HARD PART...
HEY...
JEEZ. NOT YOU, TOO. I'M FINE!

ONE, TWO, THREE!
CHK
YEEOWW!!

WHERE'S THATCH?
THATCH!
HERE HE COMES!

MOLLY AND I ARE GONNA STAY IN CASE ELRIC NEEDS ANY HELP.
GOOD DEA.
ACK!

ALL ABOARD THE HAIRY EXPRESS.
WU-WOH.
I NEED YOU TO TAKE ME TO NURSE MIM, PAL.

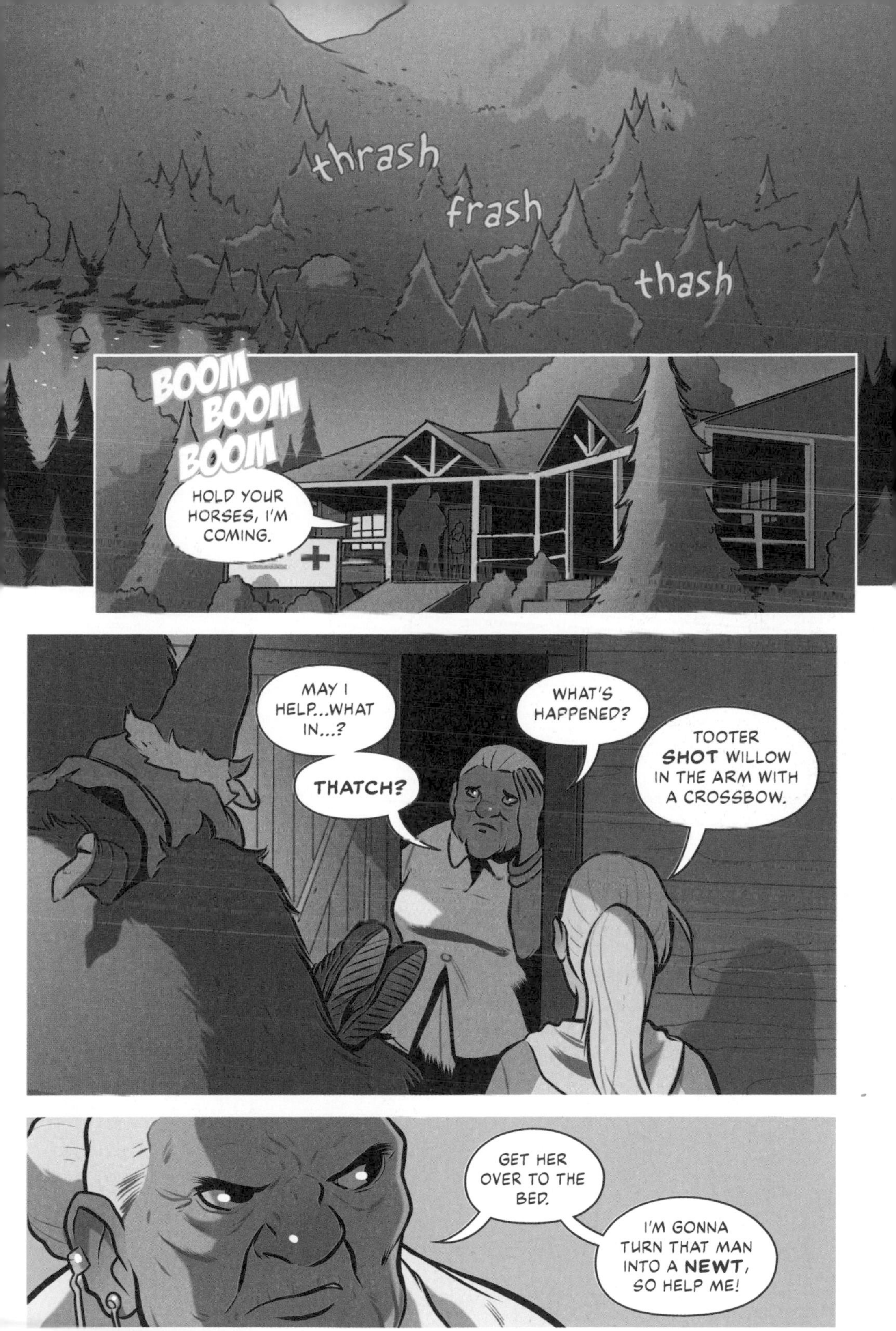

thrash
frash
thash

BOOM
BOOM
BOOM

HOLD YOUR HORSES, I'M COMING.

MAY I HELP...WHAT IN...?
THATCH?
WHAT'S HAPPENED?
TOOTER **SHOT** WILLOW IN THE ARM WITH A CROSSBOW.

GET HER OVER TO THE BED.
I'M GONNA TURN THAT MAN INTO A **NEWT**, SO HELP ME!

TRY TO RELAX, DEAR. I'VE SOME STUFF THAT'LL HAVE YOU FEELING RIGHT AS RAIN IN AN INSTANT.
THANK YOU.
TOAST, PLEASE FETCH ME MY SUPPLIES?
RIGHT AWAY!
TOAST, DEAR. NOT THOSE.
MA'AM?
MY... **OTHER** SUPPLIES.
YES, I SEE!
RIGHT AWAY!

OTHER SUPPLIES... WHAT?
SHE HAS... SPECIAL, UH... STUFF.
MIM IS KIND OF...WELL, SHE MIGHT BE A, WELL...

EMMA! YOU'RE **HERE!** I WAS WORRIED WHEN WE LEFT YOU.
I'M FINE. MOSTLY.

TOAST, TURNIP, AND I BROUGHT THE INJURED CHICKCHARNEE HERE, AND SHE HEALED IT INSTANTLY.
IT'S CRAZY.

DID SHE USE THAT ON YOUR BITE, TOO?
UH, IT'S... COMPLICATED?
I'LL BE OKAY, BUT I **MIGHT** NEED TO AVOID **WATER** FOR A WHILE.
HOLD IT STEADY.
I'M TRYING!

IS THIS WHAT YOU'RE WANTING, NURSE MIM?
YES. THANK YOU, HON.

THIS MIGHT FEEL A LITTLE STRANGE, WILLOW, BUT IT'LL FIX YOU RIGHT UP.
TONK

bloop

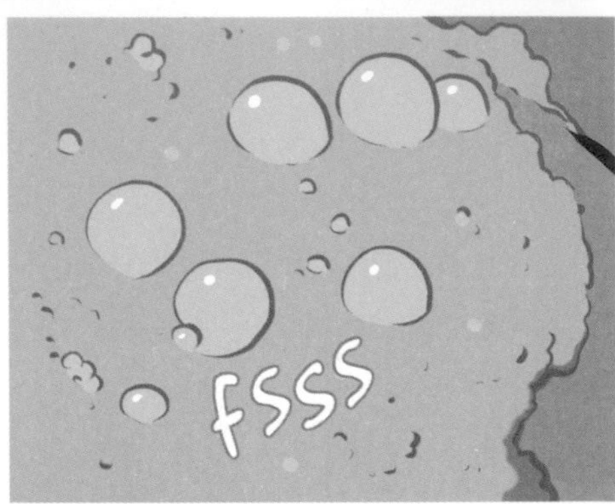
fsss

SO WEIRD!
IT ALREADY FEELS BETTER. WHAT IS THAT STUFF?

OH, JUST A LITTLE POTION I KEEP AROUND FOR EXACTLY THIS TYPE OF SITUATION.
YOU'VE GOT MEDICINE FOR WHEN SOMEONE SHOOTS SOMEONE ELSE WITH A CROSSBOW?
NOW, IT MIGHT LEAVE A SMALL SCAR, BUT NOTHING MORE.

COOL, MY FIRST SCAR!
I'M JUST RELIEVED THAT YOU'RE OKAY, WIL.
WE SHOULD PROBABLY GET YOU A NEW CAMP SHIRT THOUGH...ONE WITHOUT BLOODSTAINS.
SOUNDS LIKE YOU'VE BEEN BEING A GOOD BOY, THATCH.
HERE, I MADE YOU A GOODY BAG, BUT YOU CAN'T EAT IT UNTIL YOU'RE BACK IN THE FOREST.

OFF WITH YOU NOW, BEFORE SOMEONE ELSE DISCOVERS YOU, YA SILLY THING.

HOLD ON, THATCH.

I JUST...I WANTED TO SAY THANK YOU...FOR EVERYTHING.
WU-WOH

KISS

OH, FOR HEAVEN'S SAKE.
EVERYONE GET OUT BEFORE YOU MAKE AN OLD LADY CRY.

WELL, IT HAS CERTAINLY BEEN A UNIQUE END TO CAMP THIS YEAR, AND WE HOPE YOU'VE ALL HAD A WONDERFUL TIME.
DON'T WORRY ABOUT OUR LOST CAMPERS. WE'VE HEARD THEY'RE ON THEIR WAY BACK EVEN AS WE SPEAK.
WE'VE SPENT AN ENTIRE WEEK AT SUMMER CAMP AND I'M PRETTY SURE YOU NEVER PARTICIPATED IN ANY OF IT.
NOPE.
HEY, I THOUGHT YOU SAID THEY'D BE BACK BEFORE DARK?
LEAVE IT TO RAND TO GET LOST IN THE WOODS.
SPEAK OF THE DEVIL...
HERE THEY COME NOW, GUYS.

LOOK! HERE THEY COME NOW, SAFE AND SOUND!
IT'S ABOUT TIME.
HOORAY FOR THE CHILDRENS!

I'M BACK AND I MISSED YOU ALL SO MUCH!
FOR REAL?
clap clap
clap clap

IS...IS HE TRYING TO SMILE?
MAYBE?
I DON'T THINK HIS FACE IS SUPPOSED TO MAKE THAT SHAPE.

LET'S ALL DO THE CHOO-CHI-BOO-CHI!
GROSS, DUDE! WHAT'S ALL OVER YOUR HAND?

I TOTES FORGOT TO WASH THAT OFF.
I JUST DIDN'T CARE.

YOU GUYS!

MR. ELRIC!
I'M SO GLAD YOU'RE OKAY.
THANKS TO YOU AND YOUR FRIENDS.

IT WOULD APPEAR MIM HAS YOU ALL FIXED UP?
ALMOST LIKE NEW!

WHAT'S UP WITH TOOTER? WHY'S HE SO HAPPY?

CLARENCE AND I HAD A TALK AND, WELL...LET'S JUST SAY I CAN BE **VERY PERSUASIVE** WHEN I CHOOSE TO BE.
WHAT IF HE TELLS SOMEONE ABOUT THATCH, OR WHAT IF HE...

I'M AFRAID CLARENCE IS HAVING TROUBLE RECALLING THE EVENTS OF THE PAST WEEK. POSSIBLY DUE TO A LARGE ROCK HITTING HIM THE HEAD WHILE HE WAS SEARCHING FOR A COUPLE OF LOST CAMPERS.
IT'S ALL JUST SO **VERY** UNFORTUNATE.

YOU **HYPNOTIZED** HIM INTO BEING NICE, **AND** YOU MADE HIM FORGET EVERYTHING?

I'M AFRAID, I'VE NO EARTHLY IDEA WHAT YOU'RE SPEAKING OF.
BUT LET'S KEEP YOUR WILD THEORY JUST BETWEEN US?

MIM WOULD LIKE ME TO CHECK ON YOUR INJURY. WOULD THAT BE ALL RIGHT?
SURE.
SHE PUT A BUNCH OF SOME WEIRD BLUEISH LIQUID ON MY ARM, AND IT ALL JUST KINDA... WENT AWAY.
IT BARELY EVEN LEFT A SCAR. IT'S CRAZY.
YES... I SEE.
IT'S A GOOD THING SHE WAS HERE, OR IT COULD HAVE GONE A **LOT** WORSE, RIGHT?
UH... YES.
INDEED, WE ARE VERY FORTUNATE TO HAVE MIM AROUND WHEN THE SITUATION DARKENS.

THE NEXT MORNING
I CAN'T BELIEVE CAMP'S OVER, ALREADY.
SORRY SWIMMING DIDN'T WORK OUT FOR YOU, EMMA. I KNOW HOW EXCITED YOU WERE FOR IT.
AND NOBODY KNOWS WHAT BIT YOU, HUH?
NOT EVEN NURSE MIM?
UH... NOPE.
I DON'T KNOW WHAT MR. ELRIC SAID TO MY DAD, BUT HE'S SO HAPPY HE WANTS TO MOVE TO NOWHERE PERMANENTLY.
WELL, AT LEAST WE HAVE THE REST OF THE SUMMER TO HANG OUT, RIGHT?
YOU GUYS WANNA CHECK OUT THE ICE CREAM SHOP IN TOWN?
SURE.
TOTES.
YUM!

AM I INVITED TO GET ICE CREAM, TOO?
IT DEPENDS. ARE YOU GETTING A HAIRCUT FIRST?
HA!
OKAY, CAMPERS. LET'S BE CAREFUL AND WATCH OUR STEP BOARDING THE BOAT. WE DON'T WANT ANY LAST MINUTE BOO-BOOS.
I HOPE TO SEE YOU ALL BACK NEXT SUMMER!
HE REALLY DOES SEEM HAPPIER.
IT'S...WEIRD, BUT IT DOESN'T BOTHER ME.

I'M REALLY GONNA MISS ALL THE STRANGE AND WONDERFUL THINGS ON THIS ISLAND.
IT'S GONNA BE HARD WAITING AN ENTIRE YEAR TO RETURN.
SERIOUSLY? YOU **REALLY** DON'T HAVE A CLUE WHERE YOUR FAMILY MOVED TO, DO YOU?
WHAT ARE YOU TALKING ABOUT?
JUST WAIT UNTIL YOU GET BACK TO YOUR NEW HOME. YOU'LL SEE WHAT I MEAN.
WE'RE EVERYWHERE.
WE?
YEAH, SO REMEMBER HOW I'M A WEREWOLF?
HOW COULD I FORGET?
COOL COOL.
AND HEY, REMEMBER HOW YOU JUST SPENT AN ENTIRE **WEEK** WITH GNOMES, GOBLINS, A WITCH, BIGFOOT, A VAMPIRE, AND COUNTLESS OTHER MAGICAL CREATURES?
WAIT, A WITCH?

BUT THEY'RE STUCK ON THE ISLAND, RIGHT?
AND THE FOG LEECHES, TOO?
MAYBE YOU SHOULD ASK THE OWNER OF ROOL'S ICE CREAM PARLOR, WHILE YOU'RE THERE.
BECAUSE HE KNOWS A **LOT** ABOUT THE ISLAND?
BECAUSE SHE'S A FAUN.

THIS IS GONNA BE THE BEST SUMMER, EVER!